His Justice

His Guardians Book 4

by

Ronna M. Bacon

Proverbs 20:22

Do not say, "I'll pay you back for this wrong!" Wait for the LORD, and he will avenge you.

Table of Contents

They watched as he walked away, three teenagers bent on destruction. He wanted no part of that, he said. He had more important things to consider. He wanted to make something of himself.

The hatred towards him spewed out of the three. Rocks were picked up and thrown, missing him. Derogatory words and comments flew at his ears, wounding his heart. These were his friends, he thought. Tall and proud, he kept walking, away from a life of crime they wanted to suck him into, towards a life of freedom and honour and justice.

Running footsteps sounded behind him and then he was down, face ground into the dirt and debris. A noise came, and he was freed. Hands helped him to his feet and then into a vehicle, a cloth pressed to the deep cut near his left ear.

He stared back at the rundown apartment building he was walking away from. He should have known better than to come down here. How was he to explain to his parents what had happened?

The three watched from the dark corners of the doorway they had taken refuge in as the vehicle moved away, taking him with it. He was the bright one, the one who could figure out how to do things. Now, they were on their own. They would watch. They would follow. One day, when he was least expecting it, they would strike. He was not free of them, not by a long shot.

Chapter 1

Ian Galbraith stood outside the church building and looked around. It was a busy place that bright summer Sunday morning. The parking lot was full, and he wondered at that. There were usually parking spots available but today there were a number of extra vehicles around that looked like they belonged to a mission, His Hands Mission. He hadn't heard that this was a mission emphasis Sunday.

He turned as he heard his name. A good friend from town, Dave Allison, was striding rapidly towards him.

"Ian. Morning."

"Good morning, Dave. It's a busy place this morning."

Dave looked around, noting the vehicles, then spotting a friend and waving. "It is. It looks as if the mission team is getting ready to leave again right after the service." He stopped, then spoke to Doug Foster, who stood on Ian's other side. "Lydia's back, isn't she?"

"She is. I talked to her brother last night. She got back on Wednesday. He's heading out with the team today."

"Lydia's been away for quite a while, something like on and off for over a year." Dave nodded towards the building. "Let's grab our seat. I want to save a spot for Lydia. She usually sits with me if she's here. Is Darcy sitting with us this morning, Doug?" A glint of amusement shone in Dave's eye as he mentioned Doug's fiancée, Darcy.

He shook his head. "No, she's with Peg in the children's service this morning." He sighed. "It's becoming hard to get her to stay still long enough to sit with me in church."

"Talk to Eddie. He'll reel her in from getting too involved."

Ian started when a hand reached down beside to drop a Bible and jacket on the seat beside him. He hadn't heard anyone come behind him, but with the noise of conversation, he wasn't surprised. Dave started to stand, then sat back down at what must have been a negative movement. Ian looked behind him just in time to see a young woman moving away.

Then he felt the chill of eyes watching him. Not friendly eyes, he thought. The feeling reminded him of that day so many years ago. He swiftly scanned the area, his training kicking in. He couldn't see anyone, but he could sense their presence.

Lydia Carmichael touched her cousin on his shoulder, and he stood to let her in beside him. She sat sideways on the pew, hand lightly grasping the back, as she searched for someone.

"Have you seen Leigh?"

Dave shook his head. "Not this morning."

She sat back. "I have some stuff to give him, and I wanted to do that before the service started. They'll be away before the service ends." She rose to her feet. "There he is. I'll be right back."

Ian's puzzled eyes met Dave's. Who was she, and who was Leigh?

"That's my cousin, Lydia, Ian. She was looking for her brother. Looks like she found him."

Ian's eyes followed Lydia as she moved through the crowds, greeting friends, until she disappeared through a door. He mentally shook his head. He didn't have time to be wondering about ladies. His work kept him busy at Rebel's Elite Security Team.

Just as the service was starting, Lydia slipped back in to sit with them. Dave quietly made introductions between the two as the song leader approached the mike.

Ian listened in stunned silence at the beautiful alto coming from beside him. Dave's attention was drawn to Ian and the look on his face. He smiled to himself. Lydia was adamant that she had a horrible voice, but everyone who heard her was drawn to the strength and beauty in it.

Lydia shifted closer to Ian as they sat back down, without realizing she had. Dave looked at her with a question in his eyes.

"Greg threatened to have me go up and give an update the next time I was here. You know me, I hate that kind of stuff. Hopefully, he hasn't seen me." Her voice was low.

Dave barely kept a laugh in. "Trust me, Lydia. He knows you're here. Someone's told him."

"More than likely you."

Dave shook his head at her as Greg Evans, their pastor, approached the mike. After a few comments, he looked around.

"Lydia Carmichael, I'm told you're here this morning. I know you told me not to, but I'm sure we'd all like to have an update on the missions you've been on. I can't see you, so that means you must be hiding in the back row again." This brought laughter from the congregation; they all knew she liked the back seat. "Come on up here. Mick has your pictures, so we need you to tell us what they're about."

Ian heard Lydia sigh, then stand to make her way to the pulpit. As she stood behind the mike, the light from the stained-glass window behind her bathed her in a multi-coloured swatch. Ian tilted his head to watch, engrossed in the picture she made, not seeing the glance and raised eyebrows that Doug and Dave exchanged.

"Somehow, I knew Greg would keep his promise. He said five minutes, so you'll need to listen fast." The congregation laughed once more, knowing how fast she could talk when she was nervous.

She began to share how the Lord had worked in the various disasters they had been called to assist at, commenting on the photos as they showed on the screen behind her.

"This last one, the tornadoes that went through 500 miles north of us, it was a tough one. It's the tough ones you remember. We have verses posted in our command centre, verses that are our mission statement. Any one of you who is familiar with our group knows them."

She quoted from Matthew 25:37-40: *"Then the righteous will answer Him, saying, 'Lord, when did we see You hungry and feed You, or thirsty and give You drink? When did we see You a stranger and take You in, or naked and clothe You? Or when did we see You sick, or in prison, and come to You? And the King will answer and say to them, 'Assuredly, I say to you, inasmuch as you did it to one of the least of these My brethren, you did it to Me.'"*

"That's why we do what we do. We are called out from here to do that.

"Now, I need to tell you quickly about a couple of people who just stood out so much. Victor, where are you?" She pointed at a hand waving in the air. "You all know how much energy Victor has, how hard it is to keep up with him. The man in the next picture is 95 years old. He had his grandson drive him 1000 miles to come and help. He had so much energy we had to keep stopping him. We finally paired him up with Victor and even Victor had trouble keeping up with him. Victor told us that when he was asked why he did it, George just shrugged and said it was how he was raised, he was retired and wanted to do something, and God verbally told him to get himself over there and help.

"This is Jo and that's their house, totally destroyed. Jo is six months pregnant but hid in the bathtub with her two boys. Her husband had had emergency surgery three days before the tornado struck and was unable to get to her. She just shone with praise for how God had protected her and the boys.

"Now, the boys." Lydia's voice broke for a moment. "These two little guys, I'll never forget. Little Andrew is 5, his brother is 4. Simon Peter is his name, he'll tell you. Not Simon, not Peter, but Simon Peter. And he knows who Simon Peter in the Bible is.

"The day we left, we stopped by to see how they were doing. I sat with the boys in the dirt and debris on the street for a while. Andrew was looking around, a sadness on his face, and asked why God was so mad at their town, that He broke everything up or made it fly away.

"Little Simon Peter stood right up, face inches from his brother and sternly told him that God was not mad at them, that He had not broken their house because He was. He broke it so He could give them better stuff because He loved them so much. That's the kind of teaching that comes from children, folks. This little guy has far to go in this world. Thank you."

Greg stepped up beside her as she finished, hand on her shoulder to stop her from moving away. He was unable to speak for a few minutes, overcome with emotion, finger tapping his mouth.

Finally, he spoke, "Folks, I think that little guy, Simon Peter, just preached a better sermon this morning than I could. Lydia, I know you're home for now, but Leigh and his crew are moving out. Leigh, let's have your group stand." As the rustling stilled, Greg spoke again, "Deacons, church leaders, please stand. Find one of these folks and put your hands on them. David Knight, please lead us in prayer for these people as they head out to yet another disaster."

Lydia shivered as she sat back down beside Ian. He handed her the jacket he had picked up from the seat as a matter of habit.

She shook her head, then leaned close enough to speak in a low voice. "I'm not cold. It's just I feel something not normal here."

Ian nodded and once more looked around. She was right. There was something in the building today, something evil.

The man standing at the back of the sanctuary kept his eyes on Ian. After all these years, he had finally found him, and in a church at that. Hatred for Ian filled his heart and he had to work to keep his face neutral. He turned and walked out, sure now that he could work out the plans he had developed years ago, just waiting for the right time and place. He needed to find the other two that were in town with him.

Chapter 2

Lydia stood after the service, looking around, feeling nervous for no reason that she could think of. What had caused that feeling, she wondered?

Dave stopped beside her, eyes searching her face. He could see something was up with his cousin, but wasn't sure exactly what.

"What's wrong, Lydia?"

She shrugged. "I just don't know, Dave. Something just feels off for some reason today."

"Because it's Leigh and not you?"

"I don't think so. I just feel impending doom, as Pops used to say."

Dave nodded. Their grandfather had a whole bag of phrases and this was a common one of his.

Ian watched as she searched the area, then his eyes scanned as well. He could feel the presence of evil. He saw it enough at work, but never thought he would feel it the way he was today.

"Ian." Dave's voice broke into his thoughts. "What are your plans for lunch?"

Ian shrugged. "I'm heading back to the compound, I guess, and see what I can find."

Lydia turned to him, her gray eyes searching his face. "Come to lunch at our place. Mom always has lots. She'll need something to keep her mind off Leigh travelling today."

Dave nodded. "Exactly. Aunt Laurel always has lots. She's used to people dropping in and out."

"If you think it's okay."

"Did you drive yourself or come with someone?"

"I came with Abe, but he's headed to Eddie. I can get him to drop me off, I guess."

Dave shook his head. "Not necessary. Lydia can give you a lift. I'll go find Abe."

Lydia stared at her cousin as he spoke, then shook her head. "Come on, Ian. At least you don't have to drive with that maniac."

"Hey, I don't drive like that. Wait a minute. Which car do you have today?"

She smirked, then walked away. "Not telling."

Ian stole a glance at Dave, then spoke, "Something you need to tell me, Dave?"

Dave looked at him, then looked around, shivering. "Not about her car. I'll let her tell you. I just feel like someone is watching us, Ian."

Ian nodded. "I've had the same feeling, and Lydia mentioned it during the service." He turned to walk to where Lydia was waiting, missing the speculative look on Dave's face.

Lydia never says something like that to someone she's just met. What's up with her, Lord?

Ian stopped walking as he saw the car they were headed to. "No way! Is that yours?"

Lydia laughed, jingling the keys in her hands. "It is. It was my uncle's and when I got my license, he turned that classic beauty over to me."

Ian walked around the classic red-coloured sports car. "Nice. It must drive like a dream."

Lydia studied him, then looked around. "Here, catch."

Ian made an instinctive grab for the keys and raised his brows in a question.

"You're trustworthy. I've heard Dave and Doug talk about you for years. Go on. You can drive. Just don't tell Dave. I won't let him drive it."

Ian was shaking his head. "No, you don't know me well enough to do that." He handed her back her keys.

She shrugged. "Your loss, then."

Ian followed her into the rambling one-story home, not sure what to expect. Lydia motioned him to follow her towards the kitchen.

"Hi, Mom. I brought a stray home for you today."

Laurel Carmichael looked up from the sandwiches she was arranging on a platter and shook her head, laughing at her daughter's comment.

"You did, did you? And does your stray have a name?"

"Ian Galbraith. He's a friend of Dave's, but I think he's safe to have around. He's also one of Abe's guys."

Ian looked shocked at her words until he caught the wink she sent his way. Okay, he thought, this is going to be an interesting meal.

Lincoln Carmichael stood behind Ian, then spoke. "Behave, Lydia. I think you've been away for too long."

"Not likely, Dad. I sat with Dave this morning. He always rubs off on me."

Her father shook his head. "That he does. We need to keep you two separated. At least, Leigh's away and can't get into trouble."

Lydia shook her finger at her father, then turned to Ian. "Come on out back. We'll be eating outside. You need to find your chair and stake a claim. Knowing Mom, we'll be inundated soon with people."

"Here, take this with you, Lydia, and set it up on the big table." Laurel handed her daughter a tray, which Ian was quick to take from her.

Lydia's eyes raised to Ian's. She wasn't used to this kind of treatment. How nice, she thought.

Laurel and Lincoln watched the interchange between the two.

"What do you know about him, Lincoln?" Laurel kept her voice low.

"I've met him in the past. I don't know much more than that he works for Abe."

"I think we need to get to know him, Lincoln."

Lincoln stepped to the patio door to watch his daughter. "I suspect you're right, my dear. You could feel the sparks too, could you?"

"I could." She stopped, a sudden feeling rushing through her. "Lincoln, I don't know. I think they're both in danger."

Lincoln turned, watching his wife. "Why would you say that?"

She shrugged. "Just that premonition you're always teasing me about, I guess."

"And they're usually right on. Prayers, my dear, that's what we do."

Ian looked askance at the car Lydia was headed to. It wasn't the sports car she had driven earlier. It was an older model vehicle, looking battered somewhat.

She turned to him. "Well, come on. I said I'd give you a lift home."

"Does this thing even run?" He asked, a glint of mischief in his blue eyes.

She stopped and groaned. "Not you too. Yes, it does run. It will get us there and back. Don't worry."

Idle conversation filled the car until Lydia asked. "Do you have someone after you?"

Ian shot her a keen glance, then looked over his shoulder. "Who knows? Why?"

"We picked up a follower somewhere along the line, around the church I'd say. Though, if they're after you, how'd they know you'd be in this vehicle?"

"Sure it's not you?"

She nodded. "I don't do enemies, Ian. I pick up waifs and strays instead." She took another look in the mirror. "It's not one of your guys, that's for sure."

Accelerating as she exited the town limits, she watched. The vehicle was definitely following them.

Ian watched as she expertly shifted gears. She's good, he thought, better than some of the guys I know.

Turning down a tree-lined road, she glanced over at him as she sped along. "Ready to play some chicken?"

He stared at her, aghast. "Chicken? As in we turn around and face them?"

She nodded. "Yep."

Ian shook his head. "Really?"

At the right moment, she slammed on her brakes and spun the wheel, her car facing the oncoming vehicle, which, though a distance away, slowed.

"You're sure it's not one of your guys?" She asked again.

Ian nodded. "Yes. I've never seen that vehicle before."

"Then, hang on. I have a few tricks up my sleeve."

"That's what I'm afraid of." Ian watched as she judged her distance, hit the accelerator once more and headed for the vehicle coming towards them. Then she had slammed on the brakes, shifted gears, and headed off the road onto a narrow path that barely let their vehicle through, branches banging and scraping along the sides. She spun the wheel again and headed behind a tired old faded red barn and stopped.

Chapter 3

Ian stared at her, admiration mingling with shock at the way she had handled the vehicle. She didn't see him watching her, instead her eyes were staring out the window, just watching and waiting.

A few minutes later, they heard a vehicle slow and stop on the road, then voices approaching the barn.

"Where'd they get to? I know that was Lydia, Dave's pointed out her car enough, complaining about how beat up it is."

Ian turned to Lydia. "That's Joseph."

She nodded. "I know. Shall we?" A grin crossed her face as she pulled back around to the front of the barn and stopped.

Joseph and Micah stood there, staring at the vehicle.

"Where'd you come from?" Joseph dropped down into a crouch, so he could see in the car window.

"From behind the building. Why?"

Ian stared at her, then shrugged. "What she said. Were you behind that vehicle?"

Micah ducked his head, so he could watch them. "We were. We picked it up as we left town. Where'd you learn to drive like that?"

Lydia just smiled and shrugged. "Oh, around. I had a good teacher when I was young."

Ian knew they wouldn't get any more out of her, despite the questions that were flying at her.

"Look, guys, Lydia needs to get back to town. Let me catch a ride with you."

She stared at him, then shook her head. "Nope. When I set out to give someone a ride home, that's exactly what I do. Now, whoever owns that vehicle needs to move it, please."

Joseph watched at Lydia drove away. "She's good, Micah, although I can't believe she did what she did."

Micah agreed. "It will be an interesting conversation we have with Ian."

Joseph laughed. "Somehow, I don't think we'll learn much."

Abe Finlay watched as Ian entered the conference room for their meeting later that day. The security team was heading out on an assignment, this time close to home, to protect an overseas dignitary.

"Ian. See you made it back in one piece." Abe had heard about Ian's adventure from Joseph.

Ian mentally shook his head from thoughts of the past and looked at Abe. "I did. I didn't know she could drive like that."

Abe studied his friend and team mate. "She can. Her uncle used to drive stock cars, and Lydia and Leigh were always at the track with him, when they could be. Gregor told me once that she was a natural at it, didn't have to think through any moves she made."

"Now that, I agree with. I can see why she drives a battered old vehicle."

"That she does. That's not the reason, though. It's hers for the telling." Abe turned as the remaining six members of the team filed in.

Lydia turned from her desk as her father entered her office.

"Did you get the donations marked in?"

"I did. We're well stocked for now. I think someone will have to make a run up with more for Leigh's team, though. He called a while ago. It's worse than what they expected, or we were told."

"That's what Gregor said. He's willing to make the run if you'll work the shop for him."

"Really? I'd love to."

Her father laughed as he turned to leave. "Tomorrow then. Go see what he has on the books. You just want to get your hands dirty, that's all."

Murphy, one of Ian's team mates, slowed his vehicle to pull into Gregor's garage. Ian had left his truck there while they were away.

"Isn't that Frankie Brennan talking to the mechanic?" Murphy nodded towards the garage bay.

"It looks like him." Ian sighed. "I wonder why he's here. I just hope my vehicle's ready."

They could hear muted conversation as they sat waiting for Gregor. The door to the service bay finally opened, and Frankie entered, surprised to see them. He took a look at them, then at the closed door.

"Your vehicle's here?"

Ian nodded. "Mine. Is a problem?"

"That's what we trying to figure out." Frankie turned as the mechanic entered.

"Here you go, Frankie. I've clipped them both with as much line as I think your people will need." Lydia handed him the bags, then turned to the phone. "I'll need to replace all the lines."

Ian and Murphy stared at her, stunned to see her. Frankie started to smile. What did you do, Lydia? You didn't tell him, did you? he thought to himself as he watched Ian's face.

Lydia turned from the phone, seeing the two other men for the first time. "Hi. Ian, your vehicle. It's not ready yet. It'll be another couple of hours."

Ian stood and approached the counter, eyes thoughtful and watching. "Where's Gregor?"

"He had to head up to where Leigh is. Is there a problem?"

Ian shrugged, not sure what to say. "I'm just surprised to see you here working."

"Well, get over it. I'm fully trained and qualified. Talk to Frankie." She brushed past them and back out the door.

Ian turned to Frankie. "What's that all about?"

"Tell me, Ian, was it routine maintenance or some other reason you brought your vehicle in?"

Ian hesitated before speaking. "Routine maintenance. Why?"

Frankie tossed him the two clear plastic bags he had labelled. "Lydia found these on your brake lines. You should be thanking her."

Ian paled as he studied the objects he had caught. "What are these?"

"Not part of your brake lines, Ian. Someone wanted your lines to fail after they had found out where you were. Lydia's not quite sure what all these were meant to do, but she's sure it was to take out your brakes."

They all looked up as the door opened and a tall grey-haired man entered, looking keenly around at them.

"Gregor." Frankie's hand was out to shake that of the newcomer. "How was the trip?"

"Long and tiring. It hurts to see the devastation up there. What's going on here?"

Frankie handed him one of the bags. "Lydia found two of these on Ian's truck."

Gregor shot Ian a quick glance, then studied the object. "I haven't seen one of these in a long time. It was on Ian's truck?"

"Two of them, one on the front brake lines, the other on the rear."

Gregor nodded. "They really must have a hate on for you, Ian, to place two. One is sufficient." He walked away from them to the service bay.

The men could hear quiet voices, then Gregor and Lydia returned, very serious looks on their face.

"Ian, how many enemies do you have?" Gregor bit out the words, eyes directed at Ian.

Ian looked at Gregor, surprised at the question. "I have no idea if I have any. Why?"

Lydia walked over, grabbed his hand and plunked something down hard in it before walking away.

Ian stared at the object. "Tracking device?"

"At the very least."

Frankie reached for it. "We need to talk, Ian. This is a police matter now and we need to get to the bottom of it. How long before his vehicle's ready, Gregor? I'll need a crime scene team to go over it."

"Lydia says a couple of hours. She's waiting for parts." He turned to look at the service bay door. "I'm afraid she's going to find more of those, Frankie. She said to warn Abe to go over all the vehicles."

Frankie tapped at Caleb Logan's door. Caleb was the chief of the Riverville police department and a good friend with Frankie.

"Frankie. What do you have?" Caleb knew something was up. Frankie had been planning to leave early that day.

"This." Frankie dropped the evidence bags on Caleb's desk. "Lydia Carmichael found them on Ian's vehicle today."

"She did?" Caleb picked up one of the bags. "What did Gregor say?"

"He came in as she found the tracking device. He's seen them before but isn't saying where. I'm heading back to talk with him."

"How'd Ian take it?"

"Not well. He had no idea Lydia's a mechanic."

"It's like that, is it?"

Frankie nodded. "It certainly seems that way. Abe mentioned that she gave him a lift home one day and they had a tail. Ian got to experience her stock car driving."

Despite the seriousness of the situation, Caleb had to laugh. "I gather they had an adventure?"

"Abe said Ian was in shock that she played chicken with the vehicle following them. He couldn't give much of a description, it didn't get close enough to them. Abe also said he's never seen Ian so thoughtful about something, and they've been through a lot together."

"Lydia does that to a person." Caleb's keen eyes watched Frankie. "You say they had a tail?"

"They did. Lydia thinks they picked it up around the church, but she's not certain. What she can't figure out is how did they know Ian was with her. She had her other vehicle that afternoon."

"Now, that's interesting." Caleb sat back. "We're sure it was Ian and not Lydia?"

"Not one hundred percent. She could have made an enemy or two over the years, but I don't see that."

"I don't either. Let me know what the lab says about those and what Gregor has to add."

Chapter 4

From the front porch of his house, Abe watched as Ian restlessly paced the compound. Something's up with him, Lord, I'm just not sure what. I would say Lydia's got to him. They'd make a good couple, Lord, but Ian doesn't talk about things much. He's the quiet, steady one of the group, there when you need him the most.

Abe walked towards Ian. "Ian, something's bugging you. What is it?"

Ian turned. "I just don't get it, Abe. Who'd do that to my vehicle?"

"I have no idea, but Frankie's working on it. How about someone from your past?"

Abe watched as Ian's fingers found the faint scar near his ear. He had never said how he got it and Abe had never pried.

Ian finally shrugged. "I guess it's possible, but I'm nowhere close to where I grew up. How would they find me?"

"There are ways and means of finding people that you and I would never dream of.

Now, about your vehicle. Has Frankie said anything more?"

Ian shook his head. "No. The lab's gone over it, he said, and he's talked to Gregor. Nothing yet " He turned to Abe. "I didn't know Lydia was a mechanic. I thought she worked for the mission."

"She does both, divides her time. She hasn't been around much in the last year to help Gregor. She wanted something different to do, and loved working with him on his stock cars. Did you know she rebuilt that sports car?"

Ian looked shocked, then shook his head. "Somehow, that doesn't surprise me."

Abe started to smile, his suspicions gelling. "So, when are you going to ask her out for dinner?" An amused tone in his voice, he questioned Ian as he walked away.

Ian stood, mouth open, staring after Abe. Where'd he get that idea, Lord? I've thought about it but have gone no further. He turned towards his vehicle, halting at Murphy strode towards him, concern on his face.

"Ian, this letter came for you. It wasn't in the regular mail and it certainly doesn't look as if it was postmarked."

Ian reached for it, studying it. "I don't like this, Murphy, based on my truck. I'm heading in to see Frankie."

Ian was gone before Murphy could say anything. He hunted down Frankie at Mac's cafe, a frequent gathering spot for them all. Sliding into the booth across from him, Ian pulled out the letter.

"Murphy gave me this a few minutes ago. I haven't opened it. I'm not sure what it contains."

Frank turned the envelope over and over. "No return address. No postmark. Was it just stuck in the box?"

"That's what Murphy thinks."

"Open it, read it, and then let me have it. I'll take it to the lab. Refresh my memory. What do you do on the team, besides be the pilot when needed?"

Ian thought through what he could actually say. "I guess you could say I look after the legal end of it. I'm not a lawyer, but a paralegal. I was working towards sitting for the bar in part time studies, but that's not where my interest lies. I also do research on contacts, work on the contracts."

"So, if someone wanted to hurt Abe that way, you'd be the one they'd go after. Or else it's someone you've forgotten about in your past that's caught up with you." He nodded at the letter again. "Read it."

Ian pulled the folded paper from the envelope, hesitating before he read it. Lord, I have no idea what this is about, but You already know and know the outcome. Guide us.

He unfolded the paper and stared at the few works printed in black block lettering. His eyes raised to Frankie, and he handed over the letter.

"WE'VE FOUND YOU. NOW YOU PAY."

Frankie's eyes sought Ian's face, noting the puzzlement there. "You have no idea who this could be."

Ian started to shake his head, then stopped. "The only ones I can think of are three friends I had when I was fourteen. They were getting into crime and I wanted no part of it. I walked away." As he spoke, his fingers traced the scar.

"That's where you got that, right?" Frankie's keen eyes hadn't missed Ian's movement.

Ian nodded. "The day I walked away, they attacked me. A passerby stopped, and they ran. I didn't think they could find me though. I'm so far away from there."

"I'll get that to the lab, but I don't think we'll find much. Do you think those are the ones who followed you that day?"

Ian shrugged. "They weren't close enough for me to see or get a license plate. Besides, Lydia was too quick to make a getaway for us."

Frankie started to laugh. "That she can do. I'm sure you know she's driven stock cars since she was about 14. She's usually right up front as well. She can play dirty when she wants to."

"Now you tell me." Ian rose. "Thanks, Frankie. Appreciate your help."

Frankie watched Ian walk away and cross to his vehicle. He's heading to find Lydia, isn't he, Lord? The one everyone respects and loves, who treats everyone fairly and how You would, the big brother everyone wants to have, has fallen for his lady, even though he doesn't know it yet. They make a great couple. Deirdre, my dear, you were so right.

Ian stood at the reception counter in the mission warehouse, looking around. He had never been in there before, never having had a need to. He turned as Laurel approached.

"Ian. So nice to see you. What brings you by?"

Ian shrugged, almost in a self-conscious way. Laurel nodded to herself. He's here for Lydia. "I was looking for Lydia. I wanted to thank her for working on my truck."

"She's around back, Ian. Come through the warehouse. It's easier."

Ian's steps slowed as he approached Lydia. Frankie was talking with her and he didn't want to interrupt. Lydia's face was like a thundercloud, he thought. Definitely not happy today.

Frankie turned as he heard footsteps. Not a good time right now, Ian, he thought. She's not going to talk with you, knowing her.

Lydia looked up to see Ian nearby. She flinched, not knowing how he was going to react after what she had found.

"That's all I can think of, Frankie. Your patrol officers went through the house and so did your crime scene team. I can't find anything missing, just stuff tossed around."

"Let me know if you do. Ian." Frankie nodded as he walked away.

Ian came to a stop in front of Lydia, eyes searching her face. "Lydia, what's wrong?"

She looked up at him, anger simmering in her face and eyes. "What's wrong, you ask? I go home for a bit over lunch and find my home has been tossed. That's what's wrong."

She moved to brush by him, but his hand on her arm stopped her. Lincoln was standing at the back of the warehouse watching. Well, well, he thought, she'd never stop for us. This is interesting. Looks like you were right, Laurel, and you certainly deserve that dinner out.

Lydia looked up at Ian. "What? You want to tell me to cool it too? That's what everyone is doing."

Ian shook his head. "No. I wouldn't do that. But if you want to run away somewhere, I can help you with that. I've been taking lessons from the ladies around me. I could even fly you wherever you want to go."

She looked shocked at that. "Run? What ladies?"

He started to laugh as his arm came around her and he led her to his vehicle to tuck her inside. Once he was behind the wheel, he turned to her, laughter still in his voice. "Who should I start with? I think you know them all: Laycee, Regan, Ashling, Deidre, Rachel, Rebecca, Sarah, Elizabeth, and Adriel. Darcy found about them and decided her master's thesis would be on that. Do any of those names ring a bell?"

She stared at him, eyes wide. "They all ran away?" At his nod, she shook her head. "No way! Not all of them!"

He nodded. "All of them. Now, I came to thank you for what you found on my vehicle and fixing it. God certainly put a talent in those fingers of yours. I'm going to take you to your house if you tell me where you live, and I'll help you tidy up."

She stared at him, not sure if she had really heard him right.

He looked over at her, grin in place. "So, what's your address? Or do I have to track your parents down."

She spluttered in uncertainty, then gave it to him.

Chapter 5

Closing the door of the house behind him, Ian looked around. "I think that's the last of the garbage, Lydia. I've got it all loaded on my truck. You're sure it's okay to throw in the dumpster at the mission?"

Lydia turned, studying the tall lean man standing in front of her, sunlight playing off his red gold hair. "It is, Ian. Thank you. I dreaded coming home to this. We've cleaned as much as we can. I have someone who will come in and clean for me. She does that when I'm away."

"Can you figure out what they were after?"

Lydia shook her head as she walked back towards her kitchen with the cleaning supplies she had been using. "I have no idea, Ian, that's the thing. I don't have anything of value other than what it means to me. I'm not that kind of person to gather dust collectors."

"I can see that." Humour laced through his words. "Now that we have your home back together, come out for dinner with me."

She turned. "I don't do dinners with men, Ian, you should know that."

He inclined his head as he heard her words. "So, think of me as a friend. You do dinners with friends, don't you?"

She sighed. "Yes, that I do. Where?"

"I would say Mac's but that's a little too open for you, isn't it?"

She stood looking at him, dumbfounded that he had read her so well. "How did you know?"

He shrugged. "I just did. I'm getting to know you, Lydia, and I like what I see. You're a beauty, inside and out."

She stared at him, unsure as to how to respond. He's going there where I don't let anyone other than family close, Lord. He's found my heart already. I don't know if I can do this.

"Thank you, Ian. Now as to a restaurant, how close to town do you want?"

"It doesn't matter. You tell me where and that's where we'll go."

"Just let me freshen up and I'll be with you in about five minutes. There's a powder room at the front if you need to wash up."

Ian pulled his vehicle away from the mission building after dropping off the trash in the bin. "Okay, now give directions."

"There's this little restaurant off the beaten path, just outside of town. Great food and the building is something you won't appreciate until you see it."

Ian parked, staring at the building. "This is the restaurant? I thought it was a church."

"It used to be, but it was sold when the congregations united. It's so neat inside. They've keep the flooring, some of the pews, the raised dais. And the food is great as well. Limited menu, but that's okay."

Ian reached for her hand as they walked back out from the restaurant, not thinking of what he did as they talked. Lydia started to withdraw her hand, then nestled it back into Ian's. This is nice, she thought. He's so sweet.

"Are you heading out again soon, Ian?"

Ian shook his head. "No, we have no more travels booked now. I'm glad." He stared down at her, taking in the dark head of hair reaching his shoulder. "Abe and Murphy have switched the focus of the company now to training rather than doing actual security gigs. We're all glad."

"Oh, that must be wonderful."

Ian shut the door behind her and stood for a minute, staring around. Okay, Lord, now I know what the others meant. I can feel it, but, where are they? And who are they? Are they from my past or someone else?

"Are you okay, Ian?" Lydia questioned him as he pulled away from the restaurant.

He started to deny it, but then spoke. "Now that we've been seen together, you need to take extra precautions. That incident a couple of weeks ago, it wasn't isolated, nor were those objects and tracker you found. I had a letter come to me threatening me. I have no idea who. My fear is that they'll go after you."

Oncoming lights from behind blinded Ian in the mirror, then the vehicle was past them. He felt on edge, not sure of who was around that would want to hurt him.

Frankie stood once again in Caleb's office.

"Ian got a letter, Caleb. Nothing on it or in the wording that gives us anything to work with."

Caleb sighed. Here we go again, he thought. "Log it. With nothing to go on, we can't do much other than warn him to be careful."

"I know. I already have. By the way, he's seeing Lydia now."

Caleb's head shot up. "Of course, he is. He's in danger and he chooses now to date."

Frankie laughed. "Don't they all?"

Ian's steps slowed as he approached his truck. He stopped, watching the man hanging around it. His eyes shot around the area, searching for others, but he couldn't see any one. Cautiously, he walked on by his truck, heading down the parking lot. Stopping in front of a convenience store, he turned and waited, eyes watchful. Sudden movement to his left caused him to duck and drop the packages he held.

He gingerly picked himself up and then bent for his packages. How did he get sucker punched like that? He was better trained than that. He stood for a minute to catch his breath, seeing the lights of the emergency vehicles approaching. Someone had called the assault in and he really didn't need that. He quickened his steps and stuffing his packages in the back seat, climbed in and drove away.

Matt watched as Ian moved slowly to put the groceries away he had picked up.

"What happened, Ian?"

Ian groaned to himself. So much for getting away with it. "I had someone come at me tonight. They got my ribs."

Matt, the paramedic of the team, was instantly alert. "Did you go to Emerge?"

Ian shook his head. "No, and I won't. They'll be okay."

Matt stood in front of him, not budging. "You know better, Ian. Let me take a look at them."

Abe stood watching, questioning if this was related to the incident a few weeks ago and the letter he had heard about.

"How many, Ian?" Abe's quiet question broke the stillness.

"Two that I saw. One by the truck. The other was hiding near the convenience store. That one never said a word." Ian pulled his T-shirt back over his head. "Another thing. Lydia's place was tossed today as well."

Keen eyes watched him. "She says nothing was taken and I believe her."

"Do you think the incidents are related?"

Ian shrugged, deep in thought. Then he turned to Abe. "I don't know, Abe. I really don't know. It seems too coincidental to be anything else." He groaned as he heard Frankie's voice. "I'm out of here. Catch you later."

Frankie stood in the kitchen at Abe's, looking around. "Where's Ian?"

Abe shook his head. "He won't talk to you, Frankie."

Frankie turned. "He should. I've tracked those friends of his and they're in Oak City."

"Friends?" Abe and Matt exchanged a glance.

"He didn't tell you? Friends from his past who are looking for him is how I would put it. Now, why won't he talk to me?"

Abe exchanged another glance with Matt, then spoke. "He was assaulted tonight at the store. He won't go to Emergency. Matt took a look at him instead. Is this related to the other incidents?"

Frankie was frustrated. "How would I know if he won't talk to me? Tell him to find me tomorrow or I'll come looking for him again."

Chapter 6

The two men huddled in the rocks above Rebel's, watching. They knew Ian was there, somewhere, and they were trying to find him, to track his movements. They were making plans to get to him, somehow. He didn't stay there all the time. One of them would stay and watch for him to leave.

A man stood behind them, up the hill, watching. He had followed them from town. They weren't very quiet in their speech, he thought. Anyone could have overheard their plots and plans for the one they called Ian. His eyes raised, he studied the buildings in front of him. One day, he too would attack. But not that day. He turned and walked away.

Ian shuddered, that feeling of being watched coming over him again as he walked towards the training facility that had just been finished. Abe had set up test scenarios for them to work through.

Abe watched at Ian's eyes sought the area around him. He turned himself, searching the area of rocks and trees behind the house and surrounding the area. He loved this place, it was home, but there were times it was difficult to defend. They had had breeches before and he sighed, they likely would again. When would it stop, Lord?

Lydia turned as the man approached her in the mission reception area. He was a stranger.

"Can you tell me if you need any help? I'm looking for work."

"I'm sorry, we don't have any openings. You'll need to check with the employment office down town." She barely kept a shudder in check as he stared at her, then stared around the area, before he turned to leave. She walked to window and noted his vehicle and plate number.

"What was that all about, Lydia?" Her father stood behind her.

"It was the strangest thing, Dad. He walked in asking for work, but I would have said he was casing the place instead."

"That's interesting. Every once in a while, we have someone come through asking for work. What made him different?"

"His eyes. They were cold, dead. They looked at you but didn't see you." Lydia shuddered. "I hope he doesn't come back. Sorry, Dad, I know that's not the attitude I'm supposed to have, but he didn't make me feel safe."

"I totally understand. Warn your mom and the others. If he comes around again, I'll have a patrol officer drop by when he's here, if we can."

"I think I'll go find either Frankie or Eddie Brown and talk to them. I just don't have a good feeling about him."

"Go ahead." Her father turned to study her, seeing for the first time the apprehension she was feeling. "Do you want me to go with you?"

She shook her head. "I should be fine. I'll head to Gregor's when I finished there."

Ian took a second look. It was Lydia he saw coming back out of the police department. He headed towards her at a rapid pace, slowing when he saw someone following her. She seemed oblivious to that. She turned towards her vehicle and the man reached to grab her arm. Ian was there but not before Lydia had twisted away from the man. As Ian reached for him, the man took a look at him and then took off, disappearing in the crowds.

Ian turned back to Lydia, who stood, hands on hips, a thunderous expression on her face. "Who was that, Ian? I didn't see a thing until he grabbed me."

"No, you didn't. I was following you and tried to get to you. I was watching him. He followed you from the department. You didn't see him at all?"

She turned on him. "Don't you start! I've had enough interference in my life today."

"Don't yell at me. I didn't cause this problem, nor have I been around you today." Ian stopped, took a look around, then with a hand to her back, guided her towards his truck. "Get in. I said, get in." When she just stood there staring at him, he sighed, opened the door and scooping her up, deposited her on the seat, closing the door behind him.

He climbed behind the wheel and pulled out. She sat, mutinous expression in place, not looking at him.

"Seatbelt, Lydia." When she didn't respond, he sighed again and pulled over. Reaching past her, he pulled the belt around her and snapped it into place. *She's not making it easy, Lord. How do I reach her?*

"Feel like talking?"

She refused to look at him.

"All right. I guess we just drive around until you do. I've got the rest of the day and all day tomorrow, too." He slanted a glance at her.

She sighed. "Take me home, Ian."

"Not until you talk to me."

She stared out of the window, not responding. He finally parked where there was a view of the river and turned off the truck. The open windows let a breeze flow through.

She just sat there, not saying a word. Ian watched her, studying her face. Finally, he drove back to town, drew her out of his truck, and stood her next to her car. He stood watching her face, blank in its expression.

"I thought we were at least friends, Lydia, and I had hoped maybe someday there might be more. But obviously you're not ready to even be a friend to anyone. Your attitude needs work. You talk about what your mission stands for, but you fail to see how you treat people. It doesn't work, Lydia, not in the real world. Not with people who care about you. You've made it obvious you don't want to talk to me about anything.

That's fine. I'll walk away and leave you, that seems to be what you want. There comes a time, Lydia, when you can't do it on your own, and you need someone to be there with you. I would have liked to be him." Ian stopped, watching for a response, and seeing nothing. "Good bye, Lydia."

He turned, walked back to his truck, and reversing it, drove away, leaving her standing frozen by her car. She finally shook herself and drove away, heading for her home. Her heart had frozen at Ian's words and she didn't think it would thaw again. She just couldn't let anyone close to her. Not anyone! She was dangerous to know. If only Robert hadn't threatened her like he had. That had scared her more than she ever let anyone know. She thought she would be free of him when he was killed in that accident, but she wasn't. Lord, I need to be free, but I don't know how to get there.

They watched as she parked in her driveway, oblivious to what was around her. A few quick steps, a quick motion with a cloth, and she was unconscious and in their vehicle. They had Ian's girl. Now they could get him.

Abe watched Ian the next morning as he worked away in the office, drawing up the new contracts they had agreed they needed.

Frowning, he looked at the date. Ian wasn't to be in the office that day.

"Ian, you're not supposed to be working today." Abe's voice broke into his concentration.

"No, I'm not, but these need to be done."

"They're not urgent. I thought you knew that."

Ian sat back in his chair, staring at his computer screen. "I know they're not. I just felt like working on them."

"No, that's not what's going on. Talk to me." Abe studied Ian's profile and caught the glimpse of pain that crossed it.

"There's nothing to talk about, Abe." He rose and left, Abe staring after him.

That's not Ian, Lord, Abe thought. What happened over night?

Ian was back in the office in a short space of time. "Abe, I'm not scheduled for anything until Wednesday. Mom just called that Dad has been called back to his cardiologist on Monday. I'm flying up and be back Tuesday night."

"No problem. Let me or Murphy know if you need more time." As Ian turned to leave, Abe called him back. "Lincoln

Carmichael called a bit ago, looking for you. He wanted to know if you had seen Lydia in the last couple of days."

Ian shook his head. "Not since Wednesday. I spent a couple of hour with her without her talking to me or even looking at me. So, no, I have no idea where she would be."

"What happened, Ian?"

Ian shrugged, his eyes steady on Abe. "I have no idea. She had come out of the police department, was approached by a man in a threatening manner, then wouldn't tell me what was going on. The only thing she asked was that I take her home, and her car was right there." Ian turned and walked away, leaving Abe staring after him.

Chapter 7

Gregor stood near Lincoln, waiting for him to finish his phone conversation.

"Sorry, Gregor. I didn't think that would take so long. What's up?" Lincoln finally turned to face his brother.

"Where's Lydia? I would have thought she should have called and told me she wasn't coming into the work the last couple of days."

Lincoln froze in his movements. "She didn't come in? She didn't call you?"

Gregor shook his head to both questions. "That's not like her. If she's not coming, she lets me know."

Lincoln walked rapidly through the warehouse looking for his wife. "Laurel, have you heard from Lydia?"

Laurel turned from the photocopier. "No, I haven't, Lincoln, not for a couple of days. That's not unusual."

"Thing is, Laurel, she never showed up to work for Gregor like she was supposed to."

Laurel's hand flew to her mouth. "Oh, no, Lincoln!"

Gregor turned to head for the exit. "You two check her house. I'm headed into to talk to Frankie or Eddie."

Abe turned as Frankie approached him and frowned at the look on his face.

"I don't like that look, Frankie. What's up?"

Frankie shook his head. "That's what we're trying to find out. Is Ian around?"

"No, he's not. Why?"

"I needed to talk to him about Lydia, when he last saw her."

Abe led the way back into his office and pointed at a chair. "Ian's had to fly home today and won't be back until Tuesday. What's with Lydia?"

"That's what we don't know. No one's seen her in the last couple of days. She didn't show up at either the garage or the mission building. Her car's in the driveway at her home, purse locked inside. I was hoping Ian had seen her."

Abe shook his head. "He said he hasn't seen her since Wednesday. She had some sort of confrontation with someone that Ian walked into. She wouldn't talk to him or even look at him after that."

Frankie nodded. "That's interesting. She's usually open with how she feels. Though I must say, she has changed in the last few years."

"I had forgotten that, Frankie. She has. It seems to go back to when Robert died." Abe's attention was drawn to a plain white envelope that had only Ian's name on it sitting on top of the pile of mail. "I don't like this, Frankie. This is like the last one Ian got."

Frankie leaned forward. "No stamp, no postmark, no return address. Any way to get in touch with him to ask if we can open it?"

Abe shook his head. "Not at the moment. He's in the air somewhere."

Frankie nodded. "That's figures. Let me know when you can get in touch with him and ask if we can open that letter. I don't like it."

"I don't either, Frankie." Abe laid the letter down, studying it. "He should be on the ground in a couple of hours. I'll try then."

Lydia stirred, rolling onto her side. The smell of dirt and dust hit her full in the face, and she gagged. Her eyes flickered open and closed, not focusing. She cradled her head on her arm, wishing the dizziness and the ache would disappear. What did I do, she wondered, to end up feeling like this?

She didn't the footsteps that scraped across the carpet or feel the toe of the boot that shoved at her shoulder, sending her onto her back again. The man stood and stared down at her, then stared out the bare, dirty window. They hadn't given her that much, had they, that she still wasn't responding?

He turned, feet scraping across the carpet as if it was too much effort to pick them up. He slammed the door behind him, then went searching for the other two.

"Any word yet?" he growled, through yellowed, broken teeth.

"No yet." The man sitting at the table showed the rough life he had chosen to live, cards in front of him. "Tonight's the deadline. There's been no sign of him around that place." He squinted through the smoky haze of his cigarette. "What do we do if he doesn't come through?"

The first man snarled. "What do you think we'll do, idiot? We dump her somewhere they won't find her."

"Frankie, where are you?"

"Just leaving the office, Abe? What's up?"

Abe jumped from his truck outside the building and ran for the door. "I'm just outside. Ian called. I've opened the letter. Somehow it didn't get through before. We have until 10:00 to produce Ian or Lydia's dead."

Frankie spun as he heard Abe's footsteps behind him and pocketed his phone. "That's in what, three hours?"

Abe nodded. "It was just a fluke, or I should say God, that had Ian call. He hadn't planned to. When he heard about the letter, he had me open it. He didn't want to hear what was in though."

"He didn't? That doesn't sound like him."

Abe nodded. "Ian comes across as strong and silent, but he has a very tender heart underneath all that. This has hit him hard. I don't think Lydia realizes how much she can hurt someone without really trying. Worrying about his dad doesn't help."

"I know. We've tried to talk to her, all of us, but she doesn't get it. Now, where's that letter?"

Abe handed it over. "It looks identical to the other one."

"Come on. Eddie's around here somewhere. Caleb's gone on home, but I can reach him if I absolutely have to."

The three men laid the letter down and read it.

"10:00 P.M. SATURDAY. ELM STREET ENTRANCE TO MARINA. BY YOURSELF OR SHE DIES."

"And Ian didn't want to know what was in it?" Eddie questioned Abe again.

Abe shook his head. "No, he didn't. His mind is on his dad right now and that visit to the cardiologist on Monday. Besides, he said he spent time with Lydia the other day and she absolutely refused to talk to him. You don't do that to Ian."

Eddie turned and searched the room around him. "No one here is close to Ian's height or build. Who of your guys is, Abe?"

"Luke or Joseph. Either one is close to his height and weight, but Joseph is closer in colouring. Do you think we could really get away with this?"

Eddie shrugged. "Right now, that's all we have."

Joseph stood before Abe, dressed in one of Ian's jackets and ball caps. "Will it be enough, do you think, Abe, to fool them?"

"It's close, but we have no guarantee they'll even be there."

Joseph nodded, then turned as Frankie approached him.

"Your wire's set?"

"It is. It's an odd place to meet though, the marina at that time of night."

Eddie spoke up from where he sat on the corner of Frankie's desk. "It is strange. Not a lot of traffic. We can't set up surveillance there because of that. That's why that wire is so important." Eddie's finger jabbed at Joseph. "If we lose sight of you, that's the only thing that will keep us in touch with you. I know there are surveillance cameras, but they're directed at the boat slips, not the entrance."

Chapter 8

Joseph hunched his shoulders against the cold breeze blowing in off the water. His gaze sought the dark corners and shadows. He knew it was now after 10:00 p.m. He had been standing there for thirty minutes with no sign of anyone coming. Ian, what have you got yourself into, he asked.

"How long do you want me to wait, Eddie?"

"It's 10:30 now, Joseph. I doubt they'll be there. How about another fifteen minutes?"

"Suits me. Let me know when it's up."

By 11:00, Eddie had called Joseph back to the car and handed him a hot cup of coffee. "They didn't show anywhere around, Joseph. I'm not sure what's going on there."

"I didn't see anyone either, or for that matter, hear anyone, and I should have if there was anyone there."

"That worries me." Eddie looked back over his shoulder towards the marina. "They should have been there."

"Had anyone said anything to Lincoln and Laurel?" Joseph pulled the ball cap off and studied the monogram on it.

Eddie shook his head as he pulled away from the marina. "Frankie didn't want anyone to. He's running this, but I agreed with him. So did Caleb when Frankie called him."

"Good. I wouldn't have wanted to get their hopes up." Joseph stared out the side window at the passing lights in the store windows. "I don't get it, Eddie. This sounded like a setup or a test of some kind."

Eddie agreed. Silently he wondered what would have happened if it had been Ian there tonight. *Lord, protect our Lydia. Put a hedge around her. Bring her home safe and bring her takers to justice.*

Frankie looked up, tired lines on his face, as Eddie and Joseph sat down in his office. "They didn't show?"

Eddie shook his head. "Joseph was there for almost an hour and a half. No sign of anyone. I don't like that, Frankie."

"I don't either." He sat back in his chair, one arm extended to reach his desk, tapping the pen he held. "We have no idea who they are or why they took her."

Frankie looked up as a patrol officer stopped at his door. "I just got word they found someone down at the marina. She's alive but we don't have any identification on her yet."

Frankie was on his feet and at the door. "I may know who she is. You two stay here for now."

Frankie turned back from the ambulance as it raced away lights flashing, siren blaring, phone to his ear. He had watched as the paramedics had worked on Lydia, wrapping her in a reflective emergency blanket to try and warm her. She hadn't responded to anyone at all.

"Eddie? It's Lydia. The paramedics are on the way to the hospital with her. She's unconscious."

"I'll go find Lincoln and Laurel. You'll be tied up there for a while. Did they have any idea how long she's been there?"

"They figure sometime within the last couple of hours. Someone out walking their dog found her." Frankie turned to watch the activity behind him, spotlights brought in to brighten the area.

"So, about the time Joseph got there. This smells like a setup."

"It does. Listen, I'm needed over at the site. Let me know if you have any word. I'll be at the hospital in a while."

Lincoln and Laurel rushed through the Emergency Room doors, headed for the desk. Eddie had tracked them down and brought them in. Learning the physicians were with her, they turned to the waiting room. Nervously, Laurel perched on a chair, Lincoln pacing in front of her. Who had done this, they wondered?

Abe turned as Joseph walked into his kitchen, assessing the look on his face.

"What happened, Joseph?"

Joseph leant back against the counter. "It was a setup, Abe. Someone found Lydia dumped at the marina after I left. Eddie figures she was dumped there just before the time set for Ian to show up."

"Dumped? As in dead?"

Joseph shook his head. "No, she's alive. Frankie didn't have a lot of information on her condition when Eddie spoke to him." Joseph stared across the room, and Abe could see anger bubbling beneath the surface. "They wanted to set up Ian, Abe. Who would do that?"

Abe leaned back in his chair. "I have no idea, Joseph. I'll need to call him tomorrow or is Frankie doing that?"

"Eddie said he would. I gave him Ian's number, but I don't think Ian'll be answering if he's spending time with his parents. He usually lets it go to voice mail when he's there."

"He does." Abe shrugged. "We'll have to let it go then until he's back on Tuesday." He stared at the wall in front of him, not seeing the photos Rebecca had framed and hung there. "Dumped like so much garbage. They must really have a hate on for him."

"They've had to have been watching him, Abe. As far as I know, he hasn't known Lydia that long. He said he met her in church the day Greg had her give that missions update. And I know they've only been out once."

"Then they've been watching him close. I won't be able to wait until Tuesday to talk to him. I'll try in the morning. I have his parents' number. I may have to try that one."

Joseph nodded, then shoved himself away from the counter. "I just don't get it, Abe. Who'd be after him? I know he hasn't said much about when he was young, but he's not the type to make enemies."

"No, he's not, but there has to be something there. Go, get some sleep. Thanks for stepping in tonight."

Joseph nodded. "I just wish I had seen her."

"God knows why you didn't, Joseph. As Murphy is always telling us, God has plans and purposes for us we don't know about. This is one of those times I suspect."

Frankie sat near Lincoln and Laurel in the Emergency Department waiting room. He looked up as he heard footsteps heading their way.

Dr. John Thompson, well known and well liked in their church, was headed towards them. Lincoln stood, shook his hand and then sat back down. John sat, hesitating as to what he should say and ask.

"How is Lydia, John?" Laurel's soft voice held apprehension about what John wasn't saying.

"She's still unconscious, Laurel. It looks as if she's been drugged. No real hypothermia despite being out there in the cold wind.”

“She can’t handle drugs of any kind, John, especially anything with a sedative effect.” Lincoln spoke up. “We’ve always had to watch her. Sedatives will make her sleep for days, even just a small dose. One and only one can make her sleep for at least 48 hours.”

John nodded. “I wondered at that. We’ve drawn blood and are running panels now to see which she was given. But it makes sense.”

“Was she hurt in any way?” Laurel’s question interrupted his thoughts.

John shook his head. “No. Just the sedative effect of whatever she was given. Give us a bit, then we’ll come get you.”

John stood and looked over at Frankie, giving a small movement with his head. Frankie followed him back into the exam room areas.

“What can you tell me, John, that you didn’t tell them?”

“I had the nurse gather her clothes for you. They’re dirty and covered in fibres from whatever she was laying on. I thought you’d want them.”

"Appreciate it. Not all physicians think like you do."

"It only makes sense for you to have them to try and sort out what happened. I don't know why she was there or who did it, but find them, okay?"

"We're trying, John, but so far, we don't have much to go on at all."

Chapter 9

Ian slowly pocketed his phone and turned back to his parents' house. Abe had tracked him down on the Sunday morning. Who was it, Lord, and why Lydia? Just because of her brief association with him? Whoever it was had to have been watching him closely, Abe had commented, and Ian agreed.

Ian's father studied him over the day, finally asking him what was wrong.

Ian shrugged, then told him what had happened to Lydia.

"They have no idea?" His father's keen eyes watched his son.

"No. But Abe said it was a setup aimed at me. Joseph was there but didn't see anything, making Frankie think she was dumped before Joseph got there." Ian leaned back in on the couch, eyes studying the books on the coffee table in front of him. "I don't get it, Dad. I don't have any enemies."

"No, it's strange. The only ones I could think of was those three friends of yours you walked away from all those years ago."

Ian's startled eyes flew to his father's face. "How'd you know?"

His father shrugged. "We didn't like them, if you remember. Then you weren't hanging around them anymore. They were always in trouble, and I don't think you knew that they ended up in prison once they turned 18 because of their crimes. By that time, you were away at college. I heard they've just been released in the last two to three years. They didn't come back here. And I haven't heard where they've settled. I would think, knowing their character, they would come looking for you."

Ian nodded. "That's what I thought. I gave their names before I flew up here. I may have to go to Tracker's and see what they can come up with. Now, about you? What's your thoughts on tomorrow?"

Abe finally tracked Frankie down at the hospital.

"Frankie! I spoke with Ian this morning."

Frankie turned and waited for Abe to catch up before hitting the elevator button. "How's his dad?"

"Apprehensive but Ian says he's looking better than he has in six months and is more active. They're praying for good news tomorrow." Abe studied the floor numbers as they flashed by. "Lydia's in a room?"

"She is. I'm hoping she's awake, but Lincoln said being sedated she may not wake up for a couple of days. Sedation has that kind of effect on her."

"Wow! That's something." Abe dug through his pockets. "Ian said he had mentioned some names to you. They were friends of his back in his early teens until he walked away from them. They were really starting to get into the crime life. He also asked if I could pass the names on to Tracker."

"That won't hurt. I have no idea how they find the information they do, but they're good."

Frankie stopped in front of a room door. "Lincoln said they'd be here all day, one or the other of them."

"I won't come in, Frankie. Keep me updated, please? My guys are not happy, almost angry in fact. Ian's so well liked by everyone, they can't fathom someone doing this to him."

"That's what's bothering us too, Abe. Who and why? I don't think it's related to those incidents over the past few months directed strictly at you."

Abe stared at Frankie for a moment, then looked down the hallway, not taking in the activity around them. "That's another thought, Frankie. Who's after me, and what lengths will he go to?" He turned and walked away, leaving Frankie staring after him, lost in thought.

Someone is after our friends, Lord, and we have no idea who or why. Guide us in our investigation. Protect our friends. He stood lost in thought for a while, then shaking his head, tapped at the room door and entered.

Ian tapped at the hospital room door two days later. He had flown back early in Tuesday morning, expecting everything to be back to normal. To hear that Lydia was still in hospital was not what he had expected to hear.   And that they were not closer to catching her kidnappers was even harder to take, especially when it looked like it was directed at him. Who, Lord, he asked? Who is it? Please let them be caught before anyone is seriously hurt.

Lincoln looked up as Ian walked in. Just who we needed, Lord, and at the right time. Lydia was starting to rouse, and she wouldn't want her parents there, even though they would be. She hated the way drugs made her feel and let everyone around her know it. Maybe with Ian here, it would be different.

Lincoln rose from his chair, hand outstretched to shake Ian's, studying the younger man as he got closer. He's fighting something, Lord, and only You know what.

"How is she, Lincoln?" Ian's voice was just above a whisper.

"She's been awake on and off all day, not for long at a time though. It's takes a while for any drug to wear off." He watched as Ian's eyes traced the face of the woman lying in the hospital bed, with a softening to his eyes that he was not even aware of, but that Lincoln caught. "Listen. I just sent Laurel down to get something to eat. If you'll sit with Lydia for a bit, just to have someone with her, I'd like to join Laurel."

Ian nodded absentmindedly, not even noticing when Lincoln walked away. He approached the bed, drawing the chair closer so he could sit. Sinking down into, his eyes remained fixed on Lydia's face, drinking in the changes but also the beauty that was there. How could this have happened, he questioned again?

Lydia's eyes flickered open and closed as she roused, finally focusing on the window. Where was she? It wasn't her home. Feeling a pull at her arm, she looked. An IV, she questioned? Where….her thoughts faded as she turned to face Ian. What was he doing here? She must be dreaming, she thought.

"Hi." Ian's voice was quiet as he watched her face.

"Ian." She tried to get his name out past her dry mouth and didn't succeed all that way. She sipped from the straw in the glass of water he held for her.

"That better?" His smile finally reached his eyes.

She nodded. "What am I doing here?"

"You don't remember?"

She shook her head. "The last I remember is being at the mission and then heading into town for some reason. That reason I can't remember. Ian, why can't I?"

"Your Dad said you had headed to the police department." He watched her face as he spoke. "Someone came up to you outside the police department and grabbed your arm, but ran off when I approached you." Her eyes didn't leave his face. "You don't remember getting mad, then sitting in my truck for over two hours without looking at me or speaking to me?"

She shook her head. "No, I don't. I'm sorry, Ian. I had something happen to me in my past that can cause me to freeze when I feel threatened." She turned away from him, tears in her eyes. "Tell me I didn't freeze you out." When he remained quiet, she looked back at him. "I did, didn't I? I'm so sorry." She reached for his hand, grasping for the warmth and strength she knew she'd find. "But why am I here?"

Ian studied her face and her eyes. She really doesn't remember, does she, Lord? Thanks, Lincoln, for leaving this to me.

"You were kidnapped out of your driveway and drugged." Her mouth opened, and she shook her head. "That was last Wednesday. Today is Tuesday. Whoever took you was after me. They set up a phony meeting on Saturday night, which Joseph went to. I was out of town. Someone found you dumped at the marina and called it in."

"And I don't remember." She studied the eyes quietly watching her. "What aren't you saying, Ian?"

"I wasn't here, Lydia, when you were found. I have no idea who kidnapped you. That's something the police are working on." He stopped speaking watching her face, seeing the nuances of her expression. "What I want to know is who scared you so badly that you freeze."

She stared at him, shaking her head. "No, I can't."

"You can't, or you won't? There's a big difference there, Lydia. I want to help you."

She turned her gaze away from him, fixing it on the window and the clouds scudding through the sky. "I have never told anyone, not even my parents, what happened."

"You need to talk to someone, sweet lady, or it will haunt you for the rest of your life."

She turned back to look at him. She'd tried to move up on the bed and Ian reached for the button to raise the head of the bed. "Thank you. It's not a pretty story, Ian."

"They're usually not." He reached for her hand once again. "Tell me. I think I've heard just about everything over the years. Just tell me one thing. Did he hurt you in any way?"

She looked at him, seeing the concern in the depths of his eyes. "No. Just scared me to the point I was afraid to go out on my own." She stopped, gathering her thoughts, then looked at him. "It's sounds so simple, yet so frightening. I was part of a group of friends that used to go out for meals once in a while. There was this one fellow, not really a friend of any one of us, but he always tried to come along. One night, I ended up sitting by him. After that, he decided I was "his" girl, and he used to try and warn off all my friends. We couldn't get through to him that I wasn't "his", that I didn't want to be around him. One night, he came up behind me and grabbed my arm, trying to force me into his car. A couple of college guys came along and scared him away. The next day, we heard that as he was trying to get way, he lost control, went through a guard rail and into some trees, killing himself. Since then, I will freeze if I get scared or sometimes even startled."

Chapter 10

Ian watched her face as she finished and turned from him. His thumb rubbed the back of her hand in a soothing motion. He was at a loss for words for the minute, then spoke.

"I can imagine how scary that was for you. You're not the first one I've heard describe those feelings and reactions. They're normal. It's part of our flight or fight attitude that's within us." She turned back to watch his face as he spoke. "How can I help you get over it?"

She seemed surprised. "Why, Ian, why would you ask that?"

He shrugged. "Because no one deserves to be scared that way and to have to live that way. Because you're you and I want to help you. Because I want to get to know you better, and this is standing in our way. I'd like to explore what could be there between us. I've never met someone just like you, and I like what I see and know." He watched her eyes, frightened at first, then softening as she listened to what he was saying.

"So how do you do that, Ian? It's been a long time."

"First, God works in your heart. He's the One who makes the change, no one else. Think about it, okay? If you want to talk, call me. Here's my number." He stood and stared down at her. "Your parents should be back soon, and I need to leave. Call me, Lydia. I mean that."

She watched as he walked towards the door, tall and strong, reddish blond hair reflecting the light. Her parents were just coming back down the hall as he exited. They stopped to speak with him and then headed for her room.

Ian paced the floor of his cabin. Why had he offered to help her? He didn't have training in what she was facing. Lord, I'm over my head here. Some help would be nice. He stopped to stare out the window towards the rocks and brush behind his place. Tomorrow, he was back at work and that needed his full attention. He finally shrugged. He could do nothing about it now.

Frankie handed Eddie the new letter Abe had found. This time, it wasn't addressed directly to Ian.

Eddie opened it, read it, and then looked up at Frankie. "Is this guy for real?"

Frankie shook his head. "I have no idea what's going through his head. It's like he doesn't even care that Ian knows who he is. They certainly don't know that Lydia survived."

Eddie read through the letter again, a puzzled look on his face. "Where are the other letters, Frankie? Did you keep a copy before sending them off to the lab?"

"I did." Frankie handed over the folder he was holding. "They're here. Something struck you odd as well, didn't it?"

Eddie was silent, studying the three letters. "There's something off about this last one." He read aloud:

"YOUR LADY'S DEAD NOW, AND SO WILL YOU BE. KEEP RUNNING. WE'LL CATCH YOU. WHEN YOU LEAST EXPECT US, WE'LL BE THERE. WE'RE WATCHING YOU."

"They're admitting they're watching him. So where would they be if they're watching him?" Eddie looked up at Frankie.

"The compound. They have to be above the compound somewhere. I'll go talk to Abe and see if we can send in our search teams to track them there." He sighed. "It would be too easy if we caught them there."

"It would be." Eddie studied the letters he held again. "Has the lab come up with anything yet?"

"Nothing. When I talked to them, the tech said they must have worn gloves. There was nothing on the paper or the envelope to indicate who it was." Frank shook his head in frustration.

"That certainly doesn't help." Eddie stopped and stared at the wall in front on him, ignoring the noise he could hear. "You need to go talk to Ian. Talk to his parents as well. They may remember something Ian doesn't."

"What are we missing, Eddie? I feel like there's something there we should be seeing and we're not."

"Right now, I don't think we are. They're escalating in their threats, but haven't come right out and said how and when. That's what we're missing. Ian can't stop living. Lydia will need to watch herself as well. If they find out she survived, they'll go after her again."

Frankie shook his head at the thought and walked away, heading to talk to Abe and Ian. There had to be something we're not seeing, but what is it, Lord? I could use Your guidance and leading about now. We're at a dead end and without new evidence, we'll have to set this aside and go on to other investigations. I get that, but I don't like it. He stopped at the entrance to the compound and looked around at the rocks and shrubs surrounding it. It would be easy to hide there and not get caught, he thought. It's been done before.

He turned his head and watched as Abe walked towards him. He pulled his vehicle off to the side, parking it, and getting out to meet Abe. A few minutes of conversation, then Frankie headed back to town. Abe would have his men search the area, and if they found anything, he would call. He had a new security company in for training, and he told Frankie that it was time they got out in the real world and learned how to do things.

Abe watched as the new security team spread out, paired with one of his men, Micah staying behind to monitor the radio. He wasn't sure this was such a great idea, but these men had to start somewhere. This was part of being in security, knowing the area around them and how to search for evidence. It's not how he would have liked to stage it, but sometimes life threw a curve ball you had to work with. This was one of those times. His eyes sought for Ian and found him, heading directly for the rocks behind the house.

Ian wanted to find these men as much as Frankie and Eddie did. He felt like he was a prisoner, held hostage by someone unknown. He had finally met a lady he would like to get to know better, felt that God had brought her into his life, and had already had her hurt because of him. He wanted the man or men who had done that. Was there something in those notes he had refused to look at that only he would know? He would go find Frankie or Eddie later and find out.

"Ian!"

Ian looked up at Luke's call and saw him waving at him.

"Over here!"

"What did you find, Luke?" Ian's voice went ahead as he climbed up to where Luke stood.

"They've been here. And they have a direct line of sight down there." Luke's finger pointed at their homes. "I don't think they've been here in a couple of days, likely because we've been away."

Ian's keen eyes searched the area, stopping when he noticed shredded paper caught in the crack of a rock. "We'll need to call Frankie and get his team up here." He turned to the younger men they were training. "One thing to always keep in mind. Work with the local authorities. Never go behind their backs. If you find something like this, don't move it. Call them. That way you have their support and they have yours." The two men nodded, exchanging a glance at the vehemence in Ian's voice. Ian turned to Luke. "I'll leave you here. That way no one can say I tampered with anything."

The two men with them exchanged another glance. What had they come into to? Ian caught their glance and sighed. Abe would have to do some explaining now that this wasn't just a practice run but real life. He hated this. Why me, Lord? Why did it have to be me? I know bad things happen to Christians, but I just don't understand.

Abe studied the six men of the security team in for training that had taken seats around the table in the conference room. Murphy and Micah stood at the back of the room, leaning against the wall. This was not how the week had been planned, nor how he wanted it to get out that one of his team was targeted but he had no choice.

"Okay, fellows. Listen up. When I sent you out today, it was to be a practice run. The police had asked us to search the area around us for signs that the compound was being watched. Unfortunately, and against what I had hoped to find, we found that evidence. You have had a crash course in evidence search, not at the point in the week I would have wanted it to happen. One of my men has been the victim of someone stalking him. The police are working on that for us and so far, no one is in any danger. This goes no further, understand? It could be a matter of life and death if it does."

The six men exchanged startled glances, then looking back at Abe, all nodded. They understood only too well what could happen.

"As you can see, the police have been around today. Tomorrow, we'll pick up on where we were to be today. We'll switch the order of training around. Now, any questions?"

Ian watched as the men filed out, talking quietly among themselves. He wasn't needed for the next day's training and went to find Abe. He needed to get away for a day and wanted to let him know he would be heading out to spend some time in the air, weather permitting.

Chapter 11

Eddie looked up as Frankie approached, folder in hand. He knew Frankie had been out at Rebel's after Abe called.

"What did you find?"

"That Luke's got good eyes. He saw the evidence they had been there. Ian found the paper that was shredded. He left the area as soon as he did." Frankie perched on the corner of Eddie's desk. "I don't know how, other than God, that he found those scraps of paper. They were really hidden, whether by those men or the wind. I would suspect the wind, they seem too careless."

"Enough to figure out who yet?"

Frankie shook his head. "We're getting there. This is an earlier version of the last note. They reworked it a few times. These guys are brutal." He handed the folder over to Eddie.

"Before you read that, I talked to Ian's dad. He confirmed what Ian said about those friends of his. Ian walked away from them when he was 14. He never was around them again if he could help it, other than at school. Ian's Dad said they ended up in prison for drugs, break and enters, theft, assault. Not nice people."

"What does this one say?"

Frankie handed Eddie the folder. Eddie hesitated, sending up a prayer before he opened the folder. The note had been painstakingly patched back together.

Frankie noticed Eddie's hesitation. "It doesn't get any easy, does it?"

Eddie shook his head. "I've done this for so many years, Frankie, and lately have seen it hit too many of you that I know. I know God is in control and eventually His justice is done, but it's what you go through leading up to that, that's what gets me every time." His eyes dropped to the note and could barely contain the words that came to his lips.

"YOU SHOULD HAVE KNOWN BETTER, GALBRAITH. WE TOLD YOU WE'D CATCH UP WITH YOU, AND WE HAVE. TOO BAD ABOUT YOUR WOMAN. SHE DIDN'T DESERVE TO DIE BECAUSE OF YOU. THE NEXT ONE IS YOU."

"They're really laying it on. How do we protect Lydia now as well as Ian? If they

see she's alive, they'll come after her again."
Frankie was thinking aloud.

"Unfortunately, Frankie, there's not a lot we can do. Our hands are tied until and unless there is a direct threat at Lydia. Ian's with his team mates. They'll work on keeping him safe."

Ian stared out the window of his plane. He had needed to get away and just spend time alone in the air, just him and his God. Are you there, Lord? You know what's going on and where and when it will end. Murphy would tell me You have a plan and purpose. Dad would tell me to let it go and let You avenge, to bring in Your justice. But, Lord, they've gone after Lydia and hurt her. I want to protect her so bad.

Ian walked away from his plane after his post-flight check and headed for his truck. He had needed today to get his head back on right and to try and decide what he wanted to do about Lydia. He knew he wanted to get to know her better, but how to do that when someone was out to get him.

A voice calling his name brought him up short and he looked up to see Joseph striding rapidly towards him. Why was he here?

"Joseph! What are you doing here?"

Joseph studied his friend's face and saw the peace and relaxation there he hadn't seen in a few weeks. "Abe sent me out to find you. Frankie's looking for you."

Ian's steps slowed. "What's happened? Lydia?"

Joseph's head shook as he turned to walk back towards Ian's truck with him. "No. As far as I know, she's fine. Abe dropped me off. Frankie's pieced together those scraps of paper you and Luke found."

"I don't like the sounds of that," Ian commented as he slid behind the wheel and pulled away.

Joseph shook his head. "From what little Frankie said, I don't think you will. He wants to you head in to the department."

Ian nodded, thoughts swirling. What was going on, Lord? What had Frankie found?

Frankie looked up as someone approached. Ian and Joseph stood in front of him. He took a quick look around, then pointed at his office. Waiting for them to sit, he shut the door and perched on the corner of his desk, watching Ian's face as he did so.

"Joseph said you were looking for me, Frankie. Why?"

Frankie handed him a folder. "You refused to read any of the letters. You need to now, including the one that was found near the compound."

Ian looked at him, then down at the folder thrust into his hands. "Why?"

"Because someone's after you and also after Lydia. You're the only one who can help us. We're at a dead end. And if we don't get movement soon, this will become a cold case until either you or Lydia end up dead." Frankie didn't waste his words.

Ian shot him a startled look, staring at him for a minute, then down to the folder once again. Slowly he opened it. "Are these in any order, Frankie?"

"They're in the order they were received in. Read them, then talk to me."

Joseph watched as Ian read over the letters, his face paling, then growing stern and distant as he finished. He tapped the pages back together, then handed the folder to Joseph. "Go ahead, Joseph, read them."

He then turned to Frankie. "What do we do now, Frankie?"

"What we do now is pick your brain. I talked to your Dad. He named the same three you did. We've tracked two of them down.

Unless they're lying, and that is entirely possible, they have not been anywhere near here, no closer than Oak City and they left there quickly. All of them are miles away from your home town. We've had word the third one was killed in a prison riot." Frankie watched as Ian frowned, trying to come up with a name, any name, that would help.

"I have no idea, Frankie. I don't recognize the writing, even though they've tried to disguise it. I really don't know."

"Think, Ian. Your life depends on it. So does Lydia's. They've already proved how ruthless they can be." Frankie was pushing, and they all knew it.

Ian rose and paced what little area there was. He spun to face Frankie. "If I knew, Frankie, I would tell you. But I honestly don't know. I don't make enemies, or if I do, I don't know about it. I've wracked my brain trying to come up with names. Mom and Dad have done the same." His voice faltered and stopped. Then his phone was out, his finger in the air for them to wait.

"Hi, Mom. I have a question for you and Dad. Do you remember that fellow that decided we had taken his family home away from him? That's right. Him. Do you remember the circumstances and his name?

Dad? Did Mom tell you what I asked?" He motioned for a paper and pen. "His name again? Okay. What about family? Two boys. Two girls. His wife left him, you say? When? What happened to the kids? Okay. No, this helps. Thanks. Tell Mom I'll call tomorrow."

Ian looked up as he pocketed his phone and handed Frankie the paper he had been madly scribbling on. "This man. Try him. He maintains that Dad did something illegal and had the city confiscate his house. He owed years of taxes but had to blame someone. Dad had nothing to do with it or him. He swore he would get revenge in a way no one would ever imagine."

Frankie nodded as he took the proffered piece of paper. "We'll look into him. If you think of anyone else, call me or Eddie."

Ian nodded as he left. Who, Lord? We're coming up with names, but are no closer to who is it. Only You know. Protect us. Protect Lydia.

Chapter 12

Lydia looked around as she heard her name called. She had been thinking about Ian and his offer to help her, and here he was walking towards her. Granted, he had Joseph with him, but he was there in person, not just in her thoughts. She waited for the two men to catch up with her.

"Where are you off to, Lydia? You seem bent on a mission, pun intended." Ian's grin lit up his face. Joseph just shook his head at him.

"Mission indeed!" she replied. "I am. I have a meeting at the office about disaster preparedness. You two need to come."

Ian, with a gleam of mischief in his eyes, tossed Joseph his keys. "Joseph has to be elsewhere. I'll come." As he spoke, he reached for her hand, which nestled into his.

Joseph shook his head, a grin on his face. "Nope, I'm coming. I have to keep an eye on you two." He reached for Lydia's hand and tucked Ian's keys into it.

Lydia was laughing herself by this time. "So, I get the keys to the truck, do I?" She slipped the keys into her jeans pocket. "I think I'll keep these."

Ian shook his head at Joseph. "See what you've done? My truck will never be the same now."

Lydia laughed as she pushed open the door to the mission and headed for the conference room. "Enough, you two. I promise, I won't do any stock car racing in it."

Ian listened to the discussions going on, his sight fastened on to one particular dissenter. He tilted his head to study him further and realized he was the man that had accosted Lydia that day. Who was he, he wondered?

Ian approached Lydia after the meeting and stopped beside her.

"Who was that man that kept dissenting?"

"Him? That's George Walton. He owns one of the local newspapers. He doesn't think there is ever any problem in our town or that any disaster will ever hit."

"Is he for real?" Ian turned to scan the room for him, to find Walton's eyes glued to

Lydia with a look of hatred. "He doesn't like you much, does he?"

She shook her head. "His son wanted to date me a few years ago. I flat out refused. He's not my type."

Ian took hold of her hand and pulled her with him through the crowds, out into the warehouse where he found an empty office. He set her down on the desk and stood in front of her. "Lydia, do you remember anything about the man who I saw accost you that day?"

She shook her head, eyes fixed on his face. "Not a thing. Why?"

"Because it was either George Walton or his twin."

She looked at him and shook her head. "That can't be right. Why would he do that?"

"It was him. What does his son look like?"

"You look at George, you see his son." She stopped, horror in her face. "It was him?" At Ian's nod, she shuddered, wrapping her arms around herself. "He gives me the creeps. His son is even worse. I've heard rumours about them both, what they are involved in, and I just don't want to be around them." She stared at the floor as she digested what Ian had said.

Ian reached to draw her into his arms. "Keep away from him as much as you can. For now, you may need an escort wherever you go, including to and from work. You're not safe. He's an enemy you didn't know you had." He felt her shudder again and tightened his arms. "So, how do we do this, Lydia? How do we keep you safe?"

She tilted her head back to look up at him. "Keep me safe? How about keeping you safe?"

He shrugged. "That I don't know how we'll do it. I'm used to being at risk, with my job."

She studied his face. "But Ian, this isn't work related, is it? Are you any closer to finding out who?"

"No, we're not. Frankie's working on it, but it's becoming a cold case right now." Ian looked past her, then back down at her face. "There's nothing we've been able to find that helps us locate this person or persons."

"I don't like that." Lydia moved away from him, deep in thought. "So, how do they determine who it is?"

"They look at who I've had run-ins or problems with in the past or recently. Then they track them down, if they can find them, and question them. They look at evidence that they have. They question family and friends. A whole lot of leg work."

"It sounds like it is." She turned back to him. "Okay, so Frankie's not getting anywhere. Let's you and I tackle it."

Ian heard a noise behind him and turned to see Joseph shaking his head.

"It's not that easy, Lydia. We don't have the resources the police do."

"No, we don't, but I have a secret weapon." She pulled his keys from her pocket and slapped them into his hand on the way by. "Come on. Let's go see Gregor."

"Your uncle? Why?" Ian and Joseph had to walk rapidly to keep up with her.

"Because he has an ear to the streets the police don't have. He hears things and gets told things they don't. If he's heard anything he'll tell me, or he'll put out feelers."

"Lydia, wait." Ian reached to pull her to a stop. "How do you think your uncle will have information that Frankie won't? Wasn't Frankie a street cop?"

She nodded as she looked at the two of them. "He was, but Gregor isn't. People talk to mechanics like they do to barbers and hair stylists." She walked away towards his truck.

"She's got a point there, Ian," Joseph commented.

"Joseph, you're no help. I'm trying to keep her from doing this."

Joseph shook his head. "I know you are, and you're not going to be able to." He halted as he watched Lydia.

Ian paused, stopping beside Joseph, and staring Lydia as she stood impatiently by his truck. "That's what I'm afraid of, Joseph, that I can't stop her, and she'll get hurt."

Joseph turned to study Ian. Then he nodded. "She's got to you, hasn't she, Ian, like no one else? Is she the one?"

Ian shrugged. "I don't know, Joseph. She's special but I really don't know if she is."

Joseph laughed as he moved forward. "Everyone seems to think so, Ian. But it's your life, not ours."

Ian shook his head, then turned his eyes to Lydia. Yes, she was special, he thought, but how special remains to be seen. Lord, it's in Your hands. You lead and guide here, please.

Ian stopped his truck in front of Gregor's garage. "Are you sure he's here, Lydia?"

"No, he usually is. I don't see his truck, though. I'll see if he's said where he'll be. He was expecting me earlier today and I couldn't get there."

Ian laid a hand on her arm as she went to get out. "Lydia, we talked about this. This is one of those times we go with you. Understand?" He waited for her response. "Do you understand what I said to you?"

She gave him a mutinous look as she nodded. "I do, and I don't like it."

"You don't have to like it as long as it keeps you safe." Ian's eyes met Joseph's, who shook his head. "Lydia, you're a target and you need to keep that in mind. Do I have to talk to your Dad and get him to go with you everywhere?"

She glared at him. "No. I get it, Ian. I really do, but it's not possible for someone to be with me all the time."

"No, it's not, but if we can do that as much as we can when you're out in public, then we will. Let Joseph take a look at your home security or even Abe. They'll be able to upgrade it to keep you as safe as we can."

"At least he hasn't told you to move out to the compound where we can keep track of you better." Joseph's quiet voice with a hint of humour in it sounded from the back seat.

Lydia spun in her seat to stare back at him. "That will be the day that happens. I don't do total freedom taken away from me, just in case you didn't get it."

"We get that loud and clear, Lydia. Do you really think whoever kidnapped you before was just playing with you? They were playing for keeps." A fine edge was evident in Ian's voice, one that Joseph recognized as Ian being pushed almost to his limit. "Now, we're going in with you to the garage. One of us stays with you. Got that? Or we don't go in."

Lydia's eyes met Ian's, shock evident in them. She had not heard that tone from him before. She finally nodded. "Yes, Ian, I get it. Now, can we go in?"

Ian nodded and came around to help her out of the truck. Joseph's eyes were scanning the area, then he pointed to the back of the garage. Ian nodded.

Lydia opened up the building and started to enter. Ian stopped her with a hand to her arm.

"Let me go first, you follow me in and stand right by the door." His eyes drilled into her and she shivered at the intensity he showed.

"Okay, Ian, but you're scaring me."

"I don't mean to, but I'm glad you're scared. You'll take precautions then."

Joseph stepped through the door behind her. "All clear outside, Ian."

"The same here. Lydia, come look and see if your uncle left word where he would be. Somehow, I don't think he'd close up this early when he has cars in the bay."

She shrugged "Sometimes he does if he has to wait for parts that won't be available until the next day." She studied the work orders Gregor had on his board and desk. "That's what he's waiting for, parts for those cars out there." She looked again at his calendar. "Here. He closed early as he had an appointment. There's no surprise there as he has this appointment every two months."

Ian nodded. "Then, where will we find him?"

Lydia chewed her lip as she thought. "He might be at Mac's if he's done. If not, I don't know." She pulled out her phone and called him. "Gregor, it's Lydia. Call me when you get this. I need to talk with you."

She looked at the two men and shrugged. "Sorry, guys, this is the best I can do."

"You've tried." Ian walked towards the door. "Okay, let's get you back to the mission. Your car's there right?" She nodded. "Okay, then let's go."

Ian stopped her from getting out after he pulled up beside her vehicle. "Lydia, I'm riding with you. Joseph will follow."

She turned to him, surprise and then fear showing in her eyes. "You really mean it, don't you?"

Ian nodded regretfully. "I do. I don't like frightening you, but that's life. You need to be vigilant."

Chapter 13

Lincoln was watching for her as she stepped down from the truck and hurried towards her.

"Lydia, I know we said you were staying home for now, but we have another disaster."

"Where and when?" Lydia's full attention was on her father as they walked back towards the building.

Ian and Joseph exchanged glances, then followed them. Organized chaos were the words that came to Ian's mind. They stood back and watched, then went looking for Lydia.

"Where can we help, Lydia?"

Ian's words caught her off guard, and she stared at him for a minute, not quite catching what he said. "Oh. You want to help. Hang on a minute, OK?"

She finally turned to them. "OK. So, what do we do with you two?"

"What do you need done the most that we can do?" Ian's eyes watched her, calming her with their steady look.

"There was a serious fire in Greentown. We'll be going in to set up assistance for those left homeless. We work with the agencies already there. It looks as if we'll be pulling out late tonight." She looked back at the activity occurring behind her.

Joseph spoke up. "Where do you need us now, Lydia? That's what Ian's asking." A spark of mischief lit up his eyes. "Although if being this close to Ian when you're working a disaster makes you lose your concentration that bad, I'll take him over and ask your Dad to put him to work."

Ian glared at him as Lydia turned to look at him. Then, catching his words, she started to laugh. "No, that's not necessary. I just have so much going through my mind. With one team already away, we'll be short staffed to manage up there."

Ian stared at her. "Tell us what you need, Lydia. You're not focusing on what you have to do."

She shook her head. "No. I'm focused. I'm multi-tasking. Now, come with me. Right here. See these boxes marked personal supplies? We'll need them loaded unto skids.

The skids are right over there. I think two for now should be sufficient. Usually we go five boxes high. Then, they'll need to be wrapped with the shrink wrap. It's kept by the skids. When that's done, ccme find me."

She turned to leave as Ian reached out a hand and stopped her. "Lydia, don't leave here without either Joseph or I or your Dad. I mean it. If I even suspect that's what you're doing, I won't leave your side for a minute. Got it?"

She studied his face and nodded. "I really do get it, Ian, even though you seem to think I don't. I'll be working in this area, helping to pull supplies and organize them for the truck." She stopped, then looked past him at Joseph. "Are either of you working for the next couple of days? We're short of hands and could use you." She smirked at Ian as she added, "That way you could keep track of me."

Joseph's laughter spilled out. "She's got you there, Ian. Let me call Abe and see what's up."

Ian pulled her back towards him, a smile on his face. "You're up to no good, you know. What am I to do with you?"

She smiled. "I have no idea. Now, get to work, buster."

Ian watched her walk towards the office, then shook his head, turning to the boxes she had indicated.

Joseph helped stack the next box, then spoke. "I called Abe. He's said for us to go. The next lot of trainees aren't due for a week and he really doesn't need us right now. It's your call."

Ian gave him a quick look, then straightened to look around for Lydia. "It would solve one problem, but create another, I think."

"And that would be?" Joseph was puzzled. Here was an opportunity for Ian to spend time with the woman everyone seemed to think he was interested in and he was hesitating.

"I'm just not sure I should be around her that much, Joseph, even though I need to keep her safe. If this maniac is after me, and has already gone after her, what will be his next step? Does he follow us from town to town?"

"I don't think it really matters, Ian. He'll find either one of you wherever you are." Joseph's eyes scanned the warehouse, taking in the people moving around an orderly yet quick manner. "We don't know these people. It could easily be one of them setting it up to look like they're after you, but they're really after Lydia."

Ian stopped moving for a moment, then reached for another box. "That's what I'm afraid of, Joseph. That all this is a setup of some kind to get to her. Though why they would involve me, I don't know."

He straightened up, eyes searching the warehouse for Lydia, spotting her beside her father. "So, are you going to go with them?"

"Abe seemed to think it was a wise move if we went. Whoever it is could go after her there again."

Ian nodded as he stacked the last box on the skid, then moved to grab the plastic wrap. "He could very easily. There's always a lot of confusion at disasters, so many people milling about. Anyone could just join the crowd."

"That sounds like you've had experience with disasters."

Ian nodded. "We had some flooding one year from really heavy rains. It was horrible, the aftermath of everyone trying to help and no one in charge. I can't imagine working disasters like that all the time."

"They're trained, Ian, and Lincoln wouldn't send anyone in to a situation that he felt would get out of hand." Joseph leaned back against the skid of boxes. "I talked to him one time about how they work. He said that they always go in two pairs, two women and two men. They are never on their own or just by twos. If there aren't enough to pair up that way once the teams are set, then the people remaining don't go out. They stay where their headquarters are."

"That's reassuring. Now, let's go find out what needs done next." Ian looked up to see Abe walking towards him.

"Ian. Joseph. Looks like you've already been put to work." Abe had a grin on his face as he stopped.

"That we have, Abe. What are you doing here?" Ian studied Abe's face, trying to figure out what was up.

"After Joseph called and said the mission was short-handed, all the guys volunteered to come and help, even to going out with the mission team." Abe turned away to go find Lincoln. "Besides, they want to provide security for you and Lydia."

"Abe!"

Abe just laughed at Ian and walked away. Joseph was quick to hide his smile as Ian turned on him.

“Did you put him up to this?”

Joseph shook his head, amusement in his eyes. “Nope. He had that idea all on his own. Now, where were we?”

Ian froze in his movement forward, a horrible thought coming to him.

Joseph watched his face, then asked, “What are you thinking, Ian? I don’t like that look.”

“Just had a thought. Find Lydia. I’ll catch up with you.” Ian was pulling out his phone to call Eddie. “Eddie, can you find out something for me? That fire in Greentown that displaced so many? Do they have a cause yet?”

“I haven’t heard yet, but I’ll see what I can find out. Any particular reason you’re asking?”

“There is. His Hands mission is heading out tonight for there, and Lydia’s the lead. Anyone who’s been around the last few days would know that Leigh is still away, and Lydia would be the next one to go out.”

Eddie was silent. “Let me get on that, Ian. I’ll get back to you as soon as I can. I hate what you’re thinking.”

"Me, too." Ian thoughtfully pocketed his phone, then looked up to see Lincoln standing near him.

Lincoln approached. "I'm sorry, Ian. I wasn't eavesdropping, but you have some concerns?"

Ian's eyes scanned the warehouse, looking for Lydia. He felt relief when he saw both Joseph and Luke with her. "I do, Lincoln. We need to talk. Where can we go? I don't want to be overhead."

Lincoln looked around, then pointed to the door. "Outside is likely the best."

Chapter 14

Lincoln watched Ian's face as he gathered his thoughts, eyes in constant movement studying the area outside the warehouse.

"Okay, Ian, tell me what that was all about. Like I said, I didn't mean to eavesdrop."

Ian shook his head. "No, that's okay, Lincoln. I was coming to find you next. I asked Eddie to find out how the fire started in that building."

Lincoln's eyes narrowed as he digested what Ian had said and what he wasn't saying. "You're thinking arson?" At Ian's nod, he sighed, "Then, I know where this is going. You think that it was deliberately set, knowing we'd respond and that Lydia would be the lead. Leigh isn't back yet, and Gregor's not well enough to head up a team right now. Paul would be next, but he doesn't have the experience yet to be on his own totally."

Ian's eyes turned to Lincoln's face, seeing the conflicting emotions spreading across it. "You can't go, you're needed here. Lydia is the only one. Our whole team is going from what I understand Abe to say. That will provide some security for her, but I'm still afraid it's been a setup." Tones from his phone interrupted him.

"I don't know how you knew, Ian, but they're ruling it as arson already." Eddie's voice was frustrated. "All those people homeless. Thank God there were only a few minor injuries. If you're right and this was a setup, you need to talk to Lincoln."

"I'm with him now, Eddie. Who do we contact when we get there? Abe's here with the rest of the team, and we're all heading out with the mission team."

"Good. I'll track down the lead investigator and put you in contact with him. He'll find you once you get there."

Ian slowly pocketed his phone. This changed everything as far as he was concerned. If Lydia was the target after all, where did that put him and the letters he was getting?

"Arson?" Lincoln's voice broke into his thought.

Ian nodded. "That's what investigators are already saying, Lincoln. We don't have any connection between it and Lydia. Eddie's having the investigator connect with us once we're there." He turned back to the building. "Now, what next? I know I'll have to talk to Lydia and she's not going to be happy."

"It doesn't matter if she's happy or not, Ian. Do what you need to. Keep her safe. She has a habit of jumping in with both feet and not thinking about the consequences."

"We have spoken to her, Lincoln, both Joseph and me. We scared her earlier today and she insists she gets that she's in danger." Ian shivered, feeling the presence of evil around him. "Can I ask a favour, though? I know you do background checks on everyone. Can I get a list of names to someone who can run a check once again on everyone? I just think there's something somewhere we're missing."

"That we can do. Who are you wanting them to go to?"

"Tracker's. Either Jace or Tracker will run them for us and no one will ever know it's been done."

"I'll get Laurel to do that once you've cleared out. It locks as if you're ready to move now." Lincoln led the way back into the warehouse.

The frenzied activity was over, the trucks being loaded, and everyone was gathering in the big open area near the offices. Lincoln stepped forward, thanking everyone, giving final words of advice and comfort. Then with hands joined in a circle, he led them in prayer.

Ian looked up when Lincoln was finished. He had never experienced anything quite like that. Lydia was walking towards him with a middle-aged man he couldn't put a name to.

"Ian, this is my uncle Victor. We're riding with him in the larger truck."

"Just like that, eh? No asking? No debate?" Ian wasn't happy with her.

Victor shook his hand. "It's okay, Ian. She's told me what's been happening. I'm retired law enforcement, so we'll be good."

Ian shook his head. "Lydia should have talked to me first. Abe and the team are here, strictly to provide security for you, Lydia, at the site. We need to be involved in your decisions."

Lydia stepped back, shocked at how Ian had reacted. There was a bite to his voice she had never heard before. "But, Ian, this is what we do all the time."

Ian ran his hands through his hair in frustration. "This isn't all the time, Lydia. I've had word that the fire was arson. Who's to say it wasn't staged, knowing that His Hands would respond, and you would be there?" He looked up to see Victor nodding.

"He's right, Lydia.   It's time you stopped jumping in and doing things without checking them out. If that's all, let's get moving. It's going to be a short enough night as it is."

Lydia stared at Ian. Then, she spoke, her voice very quiet and unsure. "Do you really think that, Ian?"

He shrugged, staring off into the distance, then bringing his eyes back to her, his fear, frustration and worry in them. "I don't know, Lydia. All I know is that I have this beautiful, wonderful, compassionate, caring woman all of a sudden in my life, someone I'd like to get to know better, and all I want to do is keep her safe, and she's making it very difficult. It could be him. It might just be a coincidence. Eddie's making sure we talk to the investigator. Just stay with me or one of Abe's guys. Okay? That's all

I'm asking." As he moved, she saw the weapon he had put on under his light jacket.

"Ian, you're armed. Are all of you?" At his nod, she paled, and he reached out to steady her. "You're really serious about this, aren't you?"

"That's what we've been trying to tell you, Lydia. Someone tried to kill you and will more than likely try again. Eddie and Frankie are trying to piece it all together. Just trust us on this, okay?"

At her nod, he reached for her hand and led her over to the truck they would be traveling in. Victor approached him as he turned from helping her up and motioned him towards the back of the truck.

"I'm sorry, Ian. She didn't tell me everything."

"It's okay, Victor. I didn't think she did. Do you carry?" At his nod, Ian responded, "Good. Keep your weapon close. My team's all armed. She's been told to stay with one of us at all times."

"Good luck on that, Ian. You haven't worked a disaster with her yet."

"Oh, I think it will work. I've scared her. Besides, my team is used to working security and being fought on having it around."

Victor stopped, shock in his face. "You've scared her? That's a first. Let's get on the road. It'll be late when we get there, and we usually work through the night to get set up. We'll be coordinating with local agencies, and that can sometimes be a pleasure, sometimes a pain."

Ian looked around at the organized chaos that once more surrounded him, Abe standing beside him.

"Not like what you see on TV, is it, Ian?"

"Not at all. They never show the behind the scenes look, do they?" He paused to watch Lydia working along her uncle, Luke and Murphy beside them. "I talked to Eddie before we left."

"And?" Abe had a feeling he knew where this was headed."

"I asked him if this fire was arson. That's what they're ruling it as."

"Coincidence or deliberate to Lydia?" Abe knew how Ian thought, and he had to admit it to himself, he thought the same.

"That's what we need to figure out. He said he'd have the lead investigator connect with us."

Abe nodded. "That's good. Now, we just have to keep your lady safe."

"My lady? Why is everyone saying that?" Ian turned in time to see Abe's smile.

"Well, she is, Ian, whether you admit it or not. You've never acted this way towards anyone that I know of. What makes her the one?"

Ian shrugged. "I have no idea. Tell me, did you ask Matt, Nathaniel, and Murphy, or even Doug, the same question? Or how about Gideon?"

Abe laughed at that. "Come to think of it, I really didn't. You're different, Ian. You're a deep thinker. You don't make a move unless you've thought it through. I can see that you have by the way you're reacting to her. So can the guys. Don't worry. They're happy for you."

"Gee, thanks, Abe." Ian shook his head as he moved away, then stopped, feeling the sense of evil around him once again. "Abe, can you feel it?"

Abe nodded as he too looked around. "I can. He's here somewhere. Could he be on the team?"

"I thought of that. Lincoln's sending all the names over to Tracker's, to see what they come up with."

"They're good. If there's anything to find, they'll do it." Abe took another look at Ian. "Come on, Ian, let's go find your lady."

Ian shook his head as he moved towards Lydia. If only she would be his lady, he would be content. Lord, protect us while we're here. Help us to be Your hands over the next couple of days.

Chapter 15

Lydia turned late in that day to look around the area they had been staging their supplies. It was almost empty. She was glad they had been able to help but it had been a long day. Ian appeared at her side with a coffee for her, then took her hand and led her over to a picnic table to sit.

"You need to get off your feet. You've been on the move all day."

"Thanks, Ian. It's not usually this bad." She watched as her team moved around the area, tidying up, getting something to eat, talking with the staff from the agencies they had been working it. It had been a long day, she thought, but God had blessed them with the strength they so needed today.

"Here, you two. You need to eat." Joseph appeared beside her, plates of food in his hand.

She started to shake her head, then stopped. She really did need food. "I'm almost too tired to eat."

Ian took the plate and cutlery that Joseph handed him before Joseph seated himself on the other side of Lydia. He had spoken to the lead investigator earlier that day and heard they had the suspect in custody, a disgruntled tenant who decided the burn the building down in retaliation of being evicted. He shook his head mentally. It still didn't feel right. He could feel something out there, what he wasn't sure.

As he motioned to the left with his coffee cup, it went flying from his hand, his hand stinging as it happened. Plates of food flying, Joseph took Lydia to the ground, weapon out. Ian dropped beside them. The rest of his team were reacting, he saw, scattering the people remaining to safety and shelter.

"Go, Joseph. Get Lydia behind the truck. I'll cover you." Weapon ready as he rose, he followed Joseph as he ran with Lydia in front on him to behind the mission truck. Ian stopped just under cover and searched the area he knew the shot had come from. Nothing. Where was this guy, he thought?

"Anything, Ian?" Joseph's quiet voice came from the other side of the hood.

"No. Nothing. Abe, Luke, and Nathaniel are moving that way, but I don't think they'll find anything." Oncoming sirens grew louder before they heard the squealing of tires as brakes were slammed on. "Lydia, are you all right?"

He heard a very quiet yes from her. Great, he thought, we not only scared her, now she's come under fire and is terrified. He holstered his weapon as he saw the officers streaming into the area and turned to find Lydia and Joseph right behind him. Lydia was in his arms before he had completely turned. Joseph touched him on the shoulder as he moved past him.

"Are you okay, Ian? I thought he had shot you, you went down so fast." Lydia's arms tightened around him.

"It's how we react under fire, Lydia. We react fast and keep our people safe. Joseph didn't hurt you when he took you down, did he?" He felt her head shaking against his chest. "We're okay, sweet lady, we're okay. Come on. Let's find somewhere not so in the open for you to sit."

"How did he know to come here, Ian? How did he know?"

Ian sighed, fearful that his thoughts and ideas had been correct. "I don't know, Lydia. We don't know who it is, so we don't know how. But I suspect he was either working with that tenant or has been following one of us." He seated her at a picnic table once more and then sat beside her.

"Ian, you're bleeding!" Her words drew his attention. "Your hand!"

He looked down. She was right, he was bleeding. He looked up to see Abe and Matt approaching him, Matt taking one look at his hand and heading to find medical supplies.

"All of you okay, other than your hand, Ian?" Abe's face was impassive, eyes hard and watchful, but Ian caught the inflection in his voice.

"We are, Abe. Any sign of the shooter?"

"None. Nathaniel said he's good, whoever he is. He didn't leave a trace. We were careful moving around, didn't get close to where he was." Abe looked around at the confusion behind him. "Not the way we wanted to end our day. The investigators are going to want to talk to us. I've told Victor once they're cleared, to head out. We'll manage getting back."

Ian nodded, then watched as Matt cleaned and bandaged his hand.

"It's not bad looking, Ian. It could have been a lot worse. That cup of coffee saved your hand."

Ian nodded, feeling Lydia move closer to him. His arm around her, he thanked Matt, then watched as the lead investigator walked towards them. Vehicles connected to the mission were moving out, leaving Abe's vehicles behind.

"I don't like this, Finlay. What's going on?" The burly overweight officer faced off against Abe. Lydia figured that Abe would win, just from his calmness.

"I don't either, White. One of my men got hurt. We're here under the sanction of the mission as volunteers and also security. If you have a problem with that, take it up with the mission. We can add nothing than what we've told you." Abe didn't flinch as the man's eyes bored into his.

White turned his attention to Ian and Lydia, asking them questions again and again.

Finally, Ian had had enough. He stood pulling Lydia to her feet and walking away. "We've answered all your questions, White, in every way, shape and form you can think to ask them. If you have any further questions, get in touch with Chief Logan in Riverville and contact us through them."

"You can't just walk away." White was spluttering in his anger, rage making his hands shake.

Abe narrowed his eyes. There was something going on here, more than just an investigation into a shooting. He would have Caleb check it out.

"Yes, we can. You're finished. Next time you talk to us, it will be at our police department with our police chief and our lawyers present." Abe stared him down, then walked towards the vehicles.

Abe slammed the SUV door behind him, eyes watching the investigator he had walked away from, eyes narrowed in concentration. Murphy, at the wheel, took a look at Abe, then followed his line of sight. It was unlike Abe to slam any door. Something was up.

"All set to move out, Abe?" Murphy's voice broke into his concentration.

"Yes, we are. Let's move before he decides he's going to arrest us for something trivial."

"What was that all about, anyway?" Micah's voice sounded from the back seat. Lydia was sandwiched between him and Ian.

Abe turned. "I have no idea. He was way out of line with all those questions. Something's going on and I intend to find out what it is."

Lydia sighed, then spoke. "I can tell you a bit of why he acts like he does. He tried to volunteer with our mission, and he didn't pass the background check. He may be a police investigator, but he's had complaints made against him, and he's been up before the police discipline board before. I'm surprised to see him as an investigator."

Ian stilled, his arm around Lydia holding her close. "You know him?"

She shook her head. "No, I don't. I've never seen him before. Dad and Gregor are the ones who have had run-ins with him. We try to keep our volunteers more local to the mission and they have to pass the faith test we have in place. They represent not only our mission but our God. From what I can remember hearing, Dad didn't get a good vibe from him, and his references didn't pass the faith test."

Ian and Abe shared a look. "That doesn't explain the sniper, though." Ian commented.

"No, it doesn't." Abe turned back to the front. "I have no guarantee we'll even get a report from him."

"Let Caleb deal with his chief." Micah spoke up. "He was out of line today, and he knows it. So how do we find this sniper then, Abe?"

Abe shrugged. "I have no idea. It looks like he followed us and took advantage of a moment that came available. You saw nothing, Ian?"

Ian shook his head. "Nothing at all. I've been watching all day. But that area that he shot from. It's pretty sheltered and dark. He could have been hiding there for who knows how long and we wouldn't have seen him. He also could have managed to get a volunteer jacket and mingle with the group."

Abe paused, his heart dropping at the thought. "That's a scary thought, Ian. It's just possible that's what he did. We could have been working with him all day and never known it."

Lydia shuddered, cold in spite of the warmth coming from Ian's arm around her.

"I don't like this, guys. Find him, please, and soon."

"We're working on it, sweet lady, we're working on it. Now you understand why I was so adamant you go nowhere alone?" Ian's voice was close to her ear.

She nodded. "But it wasn't me that he was shooting at. It was you." She turned to look up into Ian's face. "And why do you always assume it's a "he"? Don't women do this kind of stuff, too? A woman would have been able to mix into the group today a lot easier than a man would. We can change appearances a lot easier, too."

Murphy saw the look on Lydia's face as he navigated his way through the town to the highway and home. She's scared, Lord, really scared. And somehow, she's managed to throw a monkey wrench into the thinking.

"She's right, you know, guys." Micah spoke up. "Who gets to tell Frankie?"

Once again, the four men shared a look. Then silence filled the vehicle, each busy with their own thoughts. Ian looked down at Lydia, who had turned into his shoulder and slept. Lord, please help me to keep her safe. Guide us to the one causing this.

Chapter 16

Abe tracked Ian down two days later, hard at work on their new contracts.

"Ian, I just got a call from Eddie." He perched on the corner of the desk, watching Ian's face.

Ian sat back. "What did he have to say?"

"He heard from that investigator we had the run in with. He claims we made up everything as he could find no evidence."

Ian choked on his mouthful of water. "We made it up?" He held up his hand. "I did this to myself?"

"Apparently. Caleb is talking to the police chief there and asking for someone to go back over everything. He's not happy with that." Abe looked down at his hands, studying them, not quite sure how to continue with what he had to say.

"Spit it out, Abe. You've got something more to say." Ian knew Abe well enough to know something was bothering him.

"There is. I talked to Eddie about Lydia's comment that it might be a female. He's willing to consider that. He asked if you had ever had any problems with women or girls in college that he needed to know about." Abe looked up to meet Ian's eyes. "I know you haven't. But he has to ask."

Ian shook his head. "Never, not that I know of anyway. I usually kept to my studies and sports. There may have been some that tried to catch my attention, but I wasn't interested in dating or even casual meals with women."

"Until now." Abe couldn't resist teasing Ian, bringing a lightening to his face.

"I agree. Until now and Lydia." Ian thought about it. "Mom might know of someone I shunned inadvertently. But it would make sense if that's the case why Lydia is targeted. But it doesn't explain the notes."

"No, it doesn't explain the notes. That's something that is puzzling everyone, those notes." Abe stared into the distance. "Those I don't get, Ian. Who'd do that to Lydia, and who would write those? The lab's not getting much from them."

"It's too bad Darcy's retired. She'd be a good one to take a look at them." Ian referred to Doug's fiancée, Darcy, a retired forensics psychologist. "I wonder if we asked, if she'd take a look at them and give us her unofficial opinion."

Abe nodded. "All we can do is ask. Let me talk to Doug and Darcy and see what they say. Doug owes me plenty of favours over the years."

Ian laughed, recalling some of the stories the two cousins had told on each other. "That he does. Maybe we could arrange a dinner out with just the four of us and see what comes up"

"You're really serious about Lydia, aren't you?" Abe wasn't surprised but felt compelled to question Ian.

"I am, Abe. It's like God brought her into my life at this moment. I have no idea where it will lead."

Abe stood, laid his hand on Ian's shoulder for a minute, then turned to walk away. "Just keep in prayer about it."

Doug looked up from his paperwork to see Ian at his door, hesitant in his manner. What's up with Ian, Doug wondered? That's not like him.

"Doug, got a minute?" Ian wasn't sure he should be there or not, but something was compelling him to talk to Doug.

"Sure, come on in. What's up?" Doug studied Ian's face.

"Abe and I were talking about what's going on, especially with Lydia. You know what's been going on?" Ian waited until Doug nodded. "You see, we have these notes and they're not making a lot of sense."

Doug nodded. "Darcy asked if you had any notes. I didn't know for sure, but thought maybe you had. I know she'd take a look at them for you." Ian looked up in surprise. "You're special to her, Ian. More so than any other of Abe's men."

"She's a special lady, Doug. How long to your wedding?"

"Next week. You'd better be around. She tells me you're walking her up the aisle."

Ian smiled. "That I am. Now, when can we can together?"

"We're having dinner tonight at her home. Bring Lydia and come for dinner. Around 6 should be good. And bring copies of those notes with you. Darcy'll want them."

"Thanks, Doug. I was hesitant to ask, knowing she doesn't do this anymore."

Doug sat back in his chair and studied Ian. "She's talking about freelancing again, while still working her online store. Abby's got the store itself running so smoothly, Darcy's not needed there."

Lydia clung to Ian's hand, uncertainty in her bearing. "Are you sure he said to come?"

"Doug did. He doesn't say something he doesn't mean. Besides, I want you to meet Darcy. Just so you know, she's asked me to walk her up the aisle at her wedding next week."

Lydia looked up at Ian. "That's sweet, Ian. But it's tonight that I'm not sure of."

Doug stood on the porch, watching them walk towards him. He shook his head. Another one, Lord, who has the lady in hand You want to make his life partner, and he really doesn't know what to do.

"Ian. Lydia. Come on in. I don't think you've met Darcy, have you, Lydia?"

Darcy stood just inside the door. "We have, Doug, but just briefly when she stopped into the store."

"That's such an amazing store, Darcy. It's doing well, I hear."

"It is. Come on in. Supper will be ready soon, but until then let's go out on the back deck and enjoy the nice weather."

Their meal completed, the two couples moved to Darcy's living room, talk general for the first while.

Then, Darcy turned to Ian. "Doug tells me you have had letters. I was curious to know if you did."

Ian nodded. "I've had some, Darcy, but I wasn't sure if you would want to see them."

Darcy shook her head and held out her hand. "If I didn't want to see them, I wouldn't ask. Now, hand them over."

Lydia watched with curiosity as Ian did just that. Why would Darcy want to see them, she wondered? Ian sat back on the couch, his arm going around Lydia and tucking her closer to him. He was unsure if this was the right move, but it was something he felt they needed to do.

"These are all of them?" Darcy questioned as she opened the folded paper. At Ian's nod, she continued, "They won't be the last. You can expect more. It is when

whoever it is goes quiet that you really have
to watch yourselves."

Chapter 17

Darcy read through the notes on the paper she had unfolded, a chill running through her that she kept hidden.

"Doug, would you get me the pad of paper and my pen from my office desk? Thank you, honey." Taking what he proffered, she read through the notes again.

"This guy's not very nice, is he?" She handed the paper to Doug.

Doug's eyes shot to Ian's after he had read the notes. "You got these? He's brutal."

Darcy spread the paper out on the coffee table and sat on the floor in front of it.

"WE'VE FOUND YOU. NOW YOU PAY."

"10:00 P.M. SATURDAY. ELM STREET ENTRANCE TO MARINA. BY YOURSELF OR SHE DIES."

"YOUR LADY'S DEAD NOW, AND SO WILL YOU BE. KEEP RUNNING. WE'LL CATCH YOU. WHEN YOU LEAST

EXPECT US, WE'LL BE THERE. WE'RE WATCHING YOU."

"YOU SHOULD HAVE KNOWN BETTER, GALBRAITH. WE TOLD YOU WE'D CATCH UP WITH YOU, AND WE HAVE. TOO BAD ABOUT YOUR WOMAN. SHE DIDN'T DESERVE TO DIE BECAUSE OF YOU. THE NEXT ONE IS YOU."

"The last one, Darcy, we never received. It was shredded and let behind our compound. We just happened to find it." Ian watched Darcy's face, searching for any hint of what she was thinking.

She nodded, then looked up. "Has Lydia seen these at all? No? Then this is all new to her as well." Darcy sat back, still staring at the paper. "I think you have more than one involved here, Ian. The "We" is used on purpose. They are really callous, aren't they? Did they leave you for dead, Lydia?"

Lydia nodded. "They did. They had kidnapped me from my driveway, drugged me, and then just tossed me away like so much garbage at the marina. Ian was supposed to be there, but he was out of town that weekend."

"That's horrible, but I've seen a lot worse." She thought about the notes. "I have some ideas, Ian, but I need to work through them. Please, both of you, be very careful. These guys are not fooling around. Call me tomorrow, Ian, and I'll let you know my thoughts." Darcy shivered, not from cold but from the thoughts running through her mind.

Ian nodded, not surprised that she would need more time. He turned to carry on a conversation with Doug. Lydia was watching Darcy and saw when she came to her conclusions.

"Darcy, do you have a moment?"

Darcy looked up, shaking off the ominous feeling she had. "Sure, come on out to the kitchen."

Lydia turned to stare back into the living room, then turned to Darcy. "You felt something just now, didn't you?"

"I did, but I'm not ready to share just yet. Come on, I want you to see my wedding dress. You do know Ian's my escort that day?"

"He told me tonight. I thought your father would be the one."

Darcy shook her head. "My parents and siblings want nothing to do with me. Ian's stepped in. You have a wonderful kind-hearted man there, Lydia."

"Not yet, Darcy, not yet. We're not anywhere close to that yet. And we may never be."

Darcy shook her head. "Ian's made up his mind. I can see it in how he watches you."

Eddie approached Caleb in the break room the next morning.

"Doug said Darcy's on her way in. Ian and Lydia talked to her last night."

Caleb turned to stare at Eddie. "They did? And she's come up with something for them, has she?"

"Doug says she has. She hasn't got to them yet. She wants to talk to us first."

"Okay. That's fair. Is Frankie in yet?"

"He is. Where do you want to meet?"

"It will have to be the conference room. Get set up for us, Eddie."

Darcy handed out the copies of material she had made. "It's not much yet, but I did talk to Tracker. She's sending over what she found from the list Lincoln sent it. She says there's a couple of names that are red-flagged and should never have made it onto the mission teams."

Caleb sat back in his chair. "How'd they get by Lincoln and Gregor?"

Darcy shrugged. "I have no idea until I see the material."

Frankie had been listening. "If there's someone there, that could explain part but not all of what's going on." He turned to the door as a tap came and accepted the folder being handed in. A quick peek at it and he nodded. "Here's Tracker's info."

He handed out the copies Tracker had made. She's good, he thought, never sending more than just one copy unless asked.

The men perused the material, sitting up straighter as they got to the names Tracker had re-flagged.

"Is she serious with these?" Doug asked as he passed his copy to Darcy.

Darcy took a look at the names. "I would say she is. It explains some of what I'm picking up, but not everything.

"Now, as to what I'm getting. They're careless and really don't care that Ian knows it. I would think it is someone he knows or who he has had contact with, likely from his teen years or early 20s. They have seen him with Lydia and have decided to get to him through her. They really don't pay attention to details. They have been watching him, from above the compound you say, Frankie?" At his nod, she continued, "They know who

144

he's working for. The last note, the one not sent, is different. It specifically names Ian. The others do not, although the third one implies that because of where Lydia was found."

She paused, for once unsure of how to explain herself. "I'm getting a lot of conflicting information here. Given what Tracker has found out about those couple of names, Lydia is also a target, but how it ties in with Ian, that's difficult to place right now. We don't have enough information. Someone needs to talk to Lincoln about what was found. When he talks to those people, I would suggest that he have one of you with him just in case of violence."

Darcy was frustrated. "I am not getting as much as I would like. Other than the letters and the incident with Lydia, has anything else happened?"

Doug nodded. "I'm sure Caleb's aware of it, but someone took at potshot at Ian when they were at the fire scene a few days ago. The investigator seems to blame Ian for it."

Caleb spoke up then. "I talked with the police chief. He's assigned a new investigator, who'll be contacting the three of them this week. He was not pleased with the conduct of that officer. Darcy, they found no evidence of who or where the sniper was actually standing. Abe's group feels that it may have been a female who could have blended in with the agencies working there."

Darcy paused, eyes going to Caleb's. Then, she nodded. "That's what has been puzzling me. There is a female involved. How, I'm not sure, but you'll likely find they are all related in some way. Ian's adamant that he has had no issues with anyone since those youths?" At their nod, she continued, "Then it will be someone who Ian has had contact with, even in a limited manner. I am at a loss here, guys. I'm just not getting a lot this time for some reason. I'm sorry. I wanted to do more for them." She sat down abruptly, scowling at the papers on the table.

"You've done what you're able to, Darcy. We haven't got much to work on either." Caleb shook his head. "That worries me. These people are going to hit again, and there will be nothing we can do to stop them."

"There's nothing coming back towards Abe this time?" Eddie questioned.

Caleb turned a thoughtful eye to him. "There hasn't been. Yet. But it can still happen and more than likely will."

"There were also those devices and trackers Lydia found on Ian's truck." Frankie spoke up.

"What?" Darcy spun to stare at him. "When was that?"

"Ian had left his truck for Gregor to look at. Lydia was working there that day. It was before she was kidnapped."

"That changes everything, guys." Darcy stood and gathered her papers. "I have to rethink all this. Catch you later."

The men stared after her as she swept from the room, then at each other.

"Did she just come up with something, Doug?" Eddie questioned.

"I think she did, but I have no idea what it could be."

Frankie caught up with Ian later that day, watching him as he walked towards him.

"Ian? Got a minute?"

Ian nodded, then looked around, uncomfortable. "I do. What's up?"

"Darcy's taken a look at what we have so far. She thinks there a woman involved in the threats."

Ian stood, stunned at the thought. "That means Lydia will be even more of a target now." He looked frustrated. "Did she give you much to go on?"

Frankie shook his head. "No, she didn't have much when we met this morning. Then she found out about the sabotage to your truck, and that sent her off on a tangent."

"I wish I knew who it was, Frankie, and could end it right now. But I really have no idea, other than what I've given you."

Frankie nodded. "We know that, Ian. What Darcy has suggested is that you've had contact with the woman in some way and she's fixated on you. You may not even know her."

Ian turned startled eyes towards him. "Now, that's a scary thought. How do you protect anyone in a situation like that?"

Frankie shrugged. "You can't. All you and Lydia can do is to take as many precautions as you can. And with Lydia, it will be difficult."

Ian shook his head. "Not any more. She's scared, Frankie, and I don't like that."

Frankie nodded, his suspicions confirmed.

Chapter 18

Lincoln turned as Eddie approached him, then handed the paperwork he was holding to Laurel. He could tell by the look on Eddie's face he wasn't there with good news.

"Where can we talk, Lincoln?"

Lincoln nodded to the door. "Out back."

Once seated at the staff picnic table, Eddie hesitated to speak.

"You've never had a problem talking to me before, Eddie. Why now?" Lincoln studied his friend.

Eddie pulled the paper from Tracker's out of his pocket. "This is why. Tracker's come back with some interesting data." He handed the paper across to Lincoln.

Lincoln took it and unfolded it to read. His face whitening, he looked up. "They made it through our search. How did they do that?"

Eddie shrugged. "Tracker's still looking into that, but she thinks there may have been a pay off or something along the lines of that."

Lincoln shook his head. "Now, the board will have to deal with this. Thankfully, these are not prominent in the mission, but still, to think they made it through all our checks and counterchecks."

Eddie nodded. "We have no idea why they did it, but we would like to talk to them."

"Does this involve Lydia in any way?"

Eddie paused at the question. "We don't know, to tell you the truth, Lincoln. We really don't know." Eddie's phone chimed, and he reached for it.

"Hang on a minute, Lincoln. That's Darcy. I want to hear what she has to say."

"Eddie, I've come up with something, and I'm really not sure who to talk to." Darcy's voice sounded strained.

"What do you have?"

Darcy spoke rapidly. Eddie's face tightened into grim lines as she spoke.

"Where's Lydia, Lincoln?" was Eddie's question when he hung up.

"She's at Gregor's. Why?"

"Call him and make sure she doesn't leave at all. Tell him we're on our way there. I'll explain when we get there."

Eddie was on the phone as they walked rapidly towards Eddie's car. He wanted to find Ian and get him to Gregor's as well.

"Abe, where's Ian?"

"He's in a training session, Eddie. He should be done in about 15 minutes."

"When he's done, get someone to bring him to Gregor's. I've just got some news I need to talk to both of them about."

"I was about to call you. Ian's received another one of those letters. He hasn't seen it yet."

"Send it in with him, please. I'll need to see it."

Abe thoughtfully studied the plain white envelope. What's in it, Lord? he questioned as he sent up prayers for his friends. Sighing, he stood to go find Ian. Who would he send with him? He mentally went over the training schedule for the day. Joseph was free. He'd go, Abe knew.

Ian looked up to see Abe approaching him, and apprehension filled him. Something was up, he could tell, just by the manner Abe was approaching him. Abe had stopped and spoken with Joseph, who had nodded and headed away.

"Abe?"

"Ian, Eddie called. He needs to talk with both you and Lydia."

"Darcy's come up with something?"

Abe wasn't surprised. "You talked with Darcy? She may have. Eddie didn't say, just said he wanted you at Gregor's asap and to send someone with you." Abe held out the envelope he had been turning over his hands. "He knows you have this and wants to see it as well."

Ian's face tightened as he reached for the envelope. "Wonder what they're threatening now. I just want this over, Abe."

"I know you do. Soon, Ian. Let Caleb and his people work it."

Ian stood, frustration in his manner. "They haven't come up with anything yet, have they?"

"Not that we know of, but they haven't had a lot to work with." Abe watched as Ian turned to leave. "Eddie hasn't said, Ian, but they may want to stick you two away somewhere."

Ian turned, surprise in his eyes. "Really?   And where would that be, I wonder?" He turned and walked rapidly away.

Abe shook his head. Ian was not being Ian today, and Abe had a suspicion it was because of Lydia. How deep are his feelings for her, Lord?

Joseph parked his vehicle outside Gregor's. "Did Abe say why here?"

Ian shook his head as he stared at the building. "No. I don't think he knew." Ian didn't move, and Joseph shot him a questioning look.

"Are you okay, Ian?"

Joseph's quiet question caught at Ian's heart. He heard what Joseph wasn't asking. "I'm not sure, Joseph. I just don't get it. I get it that God is in control, that whatever happens is for His glory and honour, but I just wish I knew what was happening." He turned to Joseph. "I just don't understand, Joseph, and that scares me."

Before Joseph could respond, a tap came at Ian's window. Frankie stood there, waiting for them to exit the vehicle. Ian opened his door, stepping down.

Frankie eyed him closely. "We were beginning to wonder if you were ever getting out."

"Don't go there, Frankie. It's bad enough you dragged me in here." Ian bit out the words, taking Frankie and Joseph by surprise. This was not the Ian they knew. Ian slapped the envelope he held at Frankie's chest. "Here's another one of those. I haven't looked at it, so I have no idea what's in it."

Frankie made a grab for the envelope as Ian walked away and into the building. He turned to Joseph, a question on his lips that died when he saw Joseph's face.

"Don't ask, Frankie. I have no idea what's going on with him, other than he's not acting like himself."

Frankie nodded. "I saw that. This is really getting to him. And I don't think what Eddie wants to talk to him about will make it any better."

"What can I do to help?" Joseph's question was so quiet that Frankie almost missed it. He turned to study the man standing before him.

"I don't know, Joseph. I know you and the rest are in prayer, but right now, we're really at a standstill. Eddie has what Darcy's been able to come up, and Lincoln has some names he's tracing back through the mission. It's frustrating. Caleb is doing his best to keep this from going to a cold case but it's heading that way." Frankie turned his eyes to study the sky, the wind picking up and sending dark clouds flying. "And it looks like we're in for a storm. That always helps."

Joseph gave a quiet laugh at that. "It always clears the air, though. That's what we want, isn't it? To clear the air?"

"Not just weather wise, Joseph." Frankie followed Joseph into the building. He stood just inside the door, back against it, and watched as Eddie spread out his paperwork across Gregor's service counter. Gregor stood behind it, one arm leaning on it, the other hand on Lydia's shoulder. Lydia was seated on a stool behind it, hands cradling her face. Ian stood nearby, his eyes on Lydia. Frankie caught the glimpse of pain and longing that swept swiftly across it. Joseph stood near a window, eyes watching out it.

Eddie looked up, then came to take the envelope from Frankie. He shot Ian a look, then opened it. His face grew even more stern as he handed it to Frankie. Frankie swiftly read it, handing it back to Eddie, before his eyes once more sought Ian and Lydia. He heard the sound of the wind picking up even more outside. A storm, he thought, is brewing, not just outside but inside. He knew that this was a defining moment for them. Would Ian stay, or would he take Lydia and run?

"Okay, Eddie, you wanted us here. Now, what is this all about?" Ian wasted no time in getting to the point. It was so out of character for him that the three who knew him best shot him a startled look.

Eddie assessed him, then nodded. Ian was angry. It didn't really show, except in the bite in his words. His eyes and face remained impassive.

"You haven't seen this last letter, Ian?"

Ian shook his head. "Abe handed to me when he said you had called this meeting." Ian stopped, drawing in a deep breath. "Do I need to see it, or can you just give me the gist of it?"

"I can do that, but I think you need to see it." Eddie walked over to him and handed him the folded paper.

Ian stared at Eddie, seeking reassurance that Eddie couldn't give. Ian sighed, then turned away from the counter and moved over towards Joseph as he opened the letter. They could see the stiffening of his back as he stopped walking.

He handed the letter to Joseph, then ran his hands through his hair. He tried to stop them shaking and couldn't. How low could someone get? And who was it?

Joseph took the letter, eying Ian as he did so. "Are you sure you want me to read this?" His voice was low enough that only Ian heard him.

Ian nodded. "I do. We'll have to talk to Abe today. He's threatening the whole team now. When and how did that change?"

Joseph's eyes questioned him. "What do you mean, Ian?"

"Read it, Joseph. Then call Abe. He needs to know as soon as we can let him know. He needs to take precautions."

Joseph unfolded the letter, eyes still on Ian. Ian had turned away from him, seeking the face of the woman he knew now he loved. How could he protect her, he wondered? Did he have to leave and take her with him, fly to some unknown area of the country? He sighed and turned back to Joseph.

Joseph's eyes finally dropped to the letter. He drew in a deep breath as he read. What kind of person would threaten like this.

"GALBRAITH, YOUR TIME IS UP, JUST LIKE IT WAS FOR YOUR WOMAN.

WHEN YOU LEAST EXPECT IT, WE WILL STRIKE, AND YOU WON'T WALK AWAY FROM US THIS TIME. YOUR FRIENDS ARE TARGETS NOW TOO BECAUSE OF YOU. HOPE YOU ENJOY SEEING THEM DIE TOO."

"Are these guys for real?" Joseph could barely get the words out.

Eddie nodded. "Afraid so, Joseph. Can you call Abe for us and let him know what's up?"

Joseph walked outside to call Abe, not wanting to tell him what the note said. Abe wasn't surprised, Joseph learned. He had been expecting something like that. He agreed that Joseph should stay with Ian for now.

Ian watched as Eddie gathered his thoughts before speaking. Where does it end, Lord, he asked? Just where does it end? We can't continue like this, living in uncertainty. His eyes turned to Lydia, tracing the beauty in her face, wondering how this would affect her.

Eddie finally looked up. "Darcy has pinpointed that there is a female involved as well as at least two males. Ian, do you know of anyone who would be after you? I know you've given names but they're not working out in the investigation."

Ian shook his head. "I'm sorry, Eddie. I know of no one else other than those I gave you. The last letter certainly sounds like those teenage friends I had, just from the wording. I walked away from them all those years ago." Ian stopped, eyes staring into the distance, as he thought about what had gone on. Then, his eyes slid shut. "I had forgotten their families. One of them had a sister, the other two a sister and brother each. Did you check out those?"

Eddie's hand froze as he was writing. "I don't know if we did. I know I didn't. Frankie, did you?"

"We gave them a preliminary look, but I don't know how deep we went. I'm on it." His phone was out, and he was speaking with one of the investigators handling the case as he exited the building.

"I need to get this last letter to Darcy." Eddie looked up at a movement from Ian.

"No, Eddie. Not now. We'll work around that. I don't want anything more to disrupt her planning and enjoyment of the next 10 days. And one thing I will say, if you or Abe or Caleb are planning on sticking us away somewhere, forget it. I've promised Darcy I'll be there for her at their wedding and I will not go back on that promise." Ian stared at Eddie, determination in his very stance.

Eddie nodded. "I get that, Ian. You'll be there. I know how important that is to Darcy and Doug both." He turned to Lydia. "Now, young lady, what are we to do with you? They think you're dead, you know."

Lydia shuddered, then nodded. "I know they do. I'm not stopping living my life just because they do. I have places to go and things I need to do. I'm not going into hiding, Eddie. You can forget that."

Eddie raised his eyes to the ceiling. "Every one of you fight us on this. And I can't say I blame you, what with the safe houses being found." He looked between the two of them. "We need to come up with a plan." He turned slightly as the door opened and both Frankie and Joseph came back in.

Frankie nodded at Eddie, who sighed. "Well, that's that, then." He turned to Ian. "Some of those relatives of the three are in the area. Frankie's trying to track their whereabouts. That does explain part of it, if it's them, and we have no guarantee it is."

Ian nodded. "Dad said the three had ended up in prison not long after they became adults." He stopped to think, puzzled at something, eyes studying the tile floor, tracing the pattern. He looked up at Eddie. "I don't understand, Eddie. Why go after Abe and the guys? Why not my parents? That would hurt worse."

Frankie froze at his words, then his eyes slid shut. "That last note. It's not connected with the other ones. It's someone different, someone after Abe. And somehow or other, he's found out about the other notes and is trying to throw us off."

Eddie turned to Frankie. "That's what we've felt all along. But who? There are two different groups here, folks, and we need to determine which one is which."

Lydia stood and walked around the counter. She stopped in front of Eddie, frustration in her manner and bearing.

"I'm not living in fear, Eddie. Nor will I not live my life as I need to. I won't stop going places and doing things, just because of whoever this is." He could see the fear in her eyes, the bravado she was using to cover it.

"We know that, Lydia. What we need to figure out is how to let you do just that." He looked over at Gregor. "Gregor, we'll need you to work with Lydia and Lincoln and come up with a schedule for her. It's not going to be forever, Lydia." Eddie turned at her protest.

Before Eddie could speak further, Ian was at her side, grasping her hand, and pulling her out the door. Ian looked around for somewhere they could talk.

"I don't want protection, Ian." Lydia was adamant in her determination. "I can't live like that."

"I know you can't. No one can." He paused near the front of Joseph's truck and watched her face. "They're just doing their job, Lydia, trying to figure out a way to make it safe for both of us."

"I know they are, Ian. I hate this." She turned from him, eyes searching the area. She could feel someone watching them, could feel the evil approaching them. All her life, she had prayed that God would send someone into her life, just for her. Ian was the very image of who she had dreamed about. Was it all to come to an end with a sniper's bullet? What had happened at the fire was just too close. Lord, what do I do? I want to honour You by working like I have been, but I'm told it's no longer safe. Guide us. Give us the wisdom we need to bring these people to justice.

"What are you planning on doing, Ian?"

Lydia's question caught him off guard. He wasn't expecting that, but should have. He looked around, trying to decide what he should tell her. He shrugged. "I'm not sure, Lydia. I need to talk to Abe. It affects us all there. I just want you to be safe." His eyes fell to her face. "What do I do, Lydia? Stay safe and put everyone at risk, or do I draw whoever this is out?"

Lydia caught her breath at Ian's words. She turned and pulled him towards the gate to the back yard of the property. Once inside, she turned to him, eyes searching his face, lingering on the scar near his ear. Was that when he got it, Lord, when he walked away from them?

Ian's eyes roamed the area at the back. He felt very uncomfortable. There were just too many places for someone to hide back here.

"Ian, do you mean that? That you would put yourself out there for someone to come after?"

He nodded. "It's what I do, Lydia. It's who I am." He looked down at her, standing in front of him, her hands on his arms. "I can't do any less for my friends and family than I do for strangers."

She nodded. "I know, Ian. That's you. But how do you stay safe?"

He shook his head. "There's not really a good option here, Lydia. No matter what we do, or where we go, or who is with us, there is a risk. We just need to take every precaution we can." He stopped, eyes once more probing the area around him. "We need to get inside, Lydia. We're too exposed out here."

She turned. "You feel it too, don't you, Ian? I feel it everywhere I go. And I felt it before I got to know you. It was around just after I came back from that last mission before Leigh left."

Ian paused, then spoke, "That was the Sunday I met you, Lydia, and we had that incident. Someone has been watching you since then."

She turned startled eyes on him. "You're right. I had forgotten. It feels like I have known you for a lot longer."

He grasped her hand to lead her back inside, then stopped, staring down at her. She looked up at him, trying to decipher the fleeting glimpse of something she saw on his face.

"Ian?" Her question was hesitant, not confident like she normally was.

"When this is all over, Lydia, I would like to spend time getting to know you in a normal manner. I would like to take you out for dinners, for walks, for coffee, just to spend time with you." Ian smiled, a gentle smile meant for her.

She studied his face more fully and then nodded. "I would like that, Ian. I really would." She sighed. "God just has to get us through this."

"He will. Now, let's see what they've come up with that I don't agree with." As they stepped through the door into the service bays, his phone rang. It was Abe.

"Ian, have they come up with a plan yet that you two aren't going to go along with?" A trace of amusement echoed in Abe's voice.

Ian groaned. "You know they have. Why would we be any different from anyone else?"

"That's what I want to hear, Ian. Listen. Bring Lydia out here for today. The guys have been discussing this and they want to talk to you both."

"Are we going to like what they've come up with?"

Abe started to laugh. "That depends. Gideon's all for you doing what he and Rebecca did. The other plans vary on that theme."

Ian shook his head as they entered the office area. "We'll see you in a bit, Abe. Tell them to stop making wild plans, okay?" He hung up on Abe's laughter.

Eddie turned as they came back in, his eyes assessing them. "So, tell me, when are you two planning to run?"

Ian shook his head. "We're not. Abe wants to talk to us. Right now, Eddie, you don't have enough to go on to warrant any more officers being involved or providing protection."

Eddie nodded, as he studied Ian's face and then Lydia's. *These two are up to something, Lord, and I'm sure I'm not going to like it when they tell me.* "What are your plans?"

"For now, I'm heading back out to Rebel's and Lydia's going with me. I need to talk to Abe." Ian's eyes met Joseph and an unspoken communication went between the two.

"It's a free country and we can't stop you. We'll let you know what we come up with." Eddie turned to walk away, then stopped. "Just stay safe, Ian, whatever it is you've planned."

"We plan on that."

Joseph watched as Eddie and Frankie paused to talk before they headed for their vehicles, then he turned back to the room. Gregor was talking quietly with Ian. Joseph walked over to where Lydia stood, a lost look on her face.

"Lydia." Joseph's voice was quiet. "Talk to me. Tell me what's up."

Lydia turned away from him. "I don't know, Joseph, I really don't know. Ian wants me to go out to Rebel's with him today, but I have so much I need to be doing here."

"Is what you're doing here something you can delegate?"

Joseph's question caught her off guard. She studied his face as she thought about it, then turned to watch her uncle. Joseph was right. She could delegate a lot of what she needed to do today and tomorrow. That wasn't the problem. The problem was that she didn't want to. She wanted to continue with what she was doing. She didn't want to give up what she enjoyed, and she was being asked to. She turned and headed for the outside door, stopping abruptly when Joseph stepped into her way.

"Remember what we talked about, Lydia? How you need someone with you?"

"Really? Here too?" At his nod, she spun and stormed out of the office into the service bays.

Ian and Gregor looked up in surprise, then turned to look at Joseph, who shrugged. Gregor headed for the bays.

"Let me talk to her, okay? Maybe I can get through to her. You'll be ready to leave in what 15, 20 minutes?"

"Sooner than that, Gregor." Ian watched as Gregor walked through the door, then turned to Joseph. "What happened, Joseph?"

Joseph shrugged, concern on his face. "She was headed for the outside and I stopped her, reminding her of what we had talked about. She took offence at that."

Ian nodded, his gaze straying to the window. "Abe and the guys have been talking. They're trying to come up with a plan." He smiled, shaking his head. "Gideon's weighing in on it."

Joseph started laughing. "I know what his plan would involve. You two aren't ready for that yet." He turned as Gregor and Lydia came back through the door, a subdued look on her face. His heart broke for his friend and his lady. How much more could they take?

Gregor nodded at Ian, then gently shoved Lydia forward. "Go with Ian, Lydia. We'll work around what we need to. I'll talk to your Dad."

Lydia turned to hug her uncle, then took Ian's hand he had stretched out for her. Gregor watched as they walked away, a heaviness in his heart. Protect them, dear Lord. Only You know what is coming. Let Your justice be done. He sighed, then turned to reach for the phone. It would not be an easy call to Lincoln. Then he stopped and instead reached for his keys, locking the door to his shop. People would understand and if they didn't that would be too bad. This was something he needed to talk to Lincoln about in person.

Chapter 20

Abe looked up from his paperwork as Joseph pushed open the office door, then glanced past him. "You did bring them with you, didn't you?"

Joseph nodded. "I did. Neither are very happy right now, though, I can tell you that." He sat, then studied Abe's face, taking in the new lines on it. Abe's taking these hard, Lord. Help us to solve this one quickly.

"I didn't think they would take it well. The guys have been brainstorming. We'll run the ideas by them and see what they think."

"If Gideon was involved, I know what his idea would be."

Abe started to laugh, his eyes filled with mirth. "Ian wasn't impressed when I told him that Gideon had a plan."

Joseph shook his head. "No, I don't think he would be. He's moving slow with Lydia." He turned his head as the door open and his team mates entered. "Ian and Lydia should be in shortly, guys. Just so you know, Lydia's fighting us every step of the way. Even Gregor talking to her didn't help. Eddie and Frankie are still tracking down leads." He turned to Abe. "Have you talked to Eddie?"

"No, I haven't had a chance. He called when I was on the other line and I haven't had a chance to get back to him. Why?" Keen eyes watched Joseph closely and caught the hesitation in his manner. "What did he say, Joseph?"

"That last note you got? It was a threat towards you and the team, Abe. Eddie feels there are two different parties writing these notes."

Abe sat back as murmurs broke out among the men. "Two different ones? That figures. How do we track down two?" Abe's eyes went to the door as it opened, and Lydia and Ian entered. Joseph moved so Lydia could have his seat. Ian stood behind her, hands on her shoulders.

"Okay, Abe, we're here. What plans and plots have you guys come up with?" Ian's greeting was typical for him and the team members relaxed a bit. "And don't tell me they all agree with Gideon."

Murphy spoke up. "Gideon has a good plan, but it's not what you're thinking. You're not ready for the step he and Rebecca took. At least, we don't think you are?" The question hung in the air for a minute, until Ian smiled and shook his head.

"Not yet, Murphy, and I don't think we'll tell you if and when we are." That brought jeers from his friends and he could feel Lydia relaxing under his hands. Good, he thought. Now let's make some plans.

"So, what is the plan Gideon has?" Ian's curiosity was high. Gideon could be very inventive when the need was there. He ran an investigative firm, but was always ready to lend a hand.

"The guys here were coming up with some pretty wild and crazy ideas, you know." Abe couldn't contain his laughter.

"And what kind of ideas would they be?" Lydia's voice was very quiet.

Abe smiled at her. "You have to understand the guys, Lydia. They joke around and make up wild scenarios, but when push comes to shove, they'll be right there to protect you."

"That still doesn't tell me what the plans were, or were you going to keep them secret until I was so wrapped up in one I couldn't refuse?" Her words had a bite to them not normal for her.

"Lydia, back off. Don't bite them. You need to understand this as well. Our guys take stuff like this very seriously and do whatever it takes to keep someone alive and safe." His hands tightened on her shoulders. "So, tell us now if you're going to go along with us or not. If you're not or aren't sure, I'm taking you back into town to your father and he can deal with you."

Lydia sat back, surprised at the tone in Ian's voice. "I'm sorry. I'm just tired and frustrated."

"We know you are, Lydia, and that's why we want to help. Don't mistake our joking around for lack of caring or compassion. It's how we relieve our stress."

She nodded. "Okay, as Ian says, what are the plans?"

Abe studied her before he spoke, eyes going to the men standing around the room and then to Ian's face. Ian was looking down at Lydia and missed the speculative glances Abe gave him.

"So, these are the plans. Gideon thought you two should elope and come back when it was all over. The other guys wouldn't quite agree on that as they knew Ian would never stay away. What the consensus was…" Here he paused, not quite sure how to continue.

Ian waited, then sighed. "Spit it out, Abe. I really want to know what the consensus was." He could hear quiet laughter behind him.

"You're sure on that, Ian?" Eyes steady, Abe watched his face, not quite keeping the small smile hidden.

"Yes, I do." Ian turned to look at his team mates. "And I already know I'm not going to like it."

Murphy shook his head. "He hasn't even heard it yet and he doesn't like it. Where did we go wrong, boys?"

Laughter broke out at that, startling Lydia. Ian's hands tightened on her shoulders once again.

"Okay, Ian, we'll share." Abe studied the couple in front of him. Lord, how do we keep them safe and alive when we don't even know who we're fighting? Only You can. "This is what we've come up with. Ian, you're not training every day or working in the office every day. Some of what you do you can do off site on your laptop. We recommend those are the days you spend with Lydia. We've reworked our schedules so that one of the other guys is always free on the days you are. When you do have to be on site training, two of our guys are freed up to spend the day with Lydia. Unless of course she wants to spend all her days here?”

Abe grinned as she shook her head. “No, absolutely not. Not that I don’t like you guys, but I need to keep busy.”

“We know that, Lydia. That’s why we’re taking the steps we are to keep you and Ian safe. You’ll have someone with you every day. In the evenings and at night, for now, we recommend you spend it at your parents.” He held up a hand at her protest. “Either that, or we set you up here and that means bringing Rebecca and Gideon back into the main house, which they will do, but I would rather we didn’t.”

She stood and moved to the door. “I need to think about this and pray about it.” Joseph moved to stop her from opening the door. “You mean, even here I have to have someone with me?” She spun to face Abe. “Isn’t it safe even here?”

“We don’t want to take a chance, Lydia. Our area has been breached in the past.”

Joseph watched with compassion as she stopped, tears in her eyes, shaking her head. She was out the door before he could stop her, Ian right after her.

Abe looked at the door, then at his team. "Well, guys, I have no idea what the next step is. Let's stand down for now, until Ian can talk to her. I still think this is the best plan we can come up with."

Luke spoke up. "It is, Abe, but it's hard for her to give up her freedom even for a while, and we have no way of knowing how long this will go on for."

"That's the problem, isn't it?" Micah spoke from the far side of the room. "We don't know how long this will go on for, and I know she likely doesn't want to tie us up for long."

Abe thought about what had been said and frankly had to agree. He watched as the men left, frustration in him that they were no closer to a solution.

Chapter 21

Ten days later, Lydia settled down into the pew Joseph had escorted her to. Murphy finally reached and laid his hand on hers as she moved restlessly.

"Relax, Lydia." he said as his fiancée, Adriel, peeked around him at her with a smile.

"I shouldn't be sitting here." Lydia was stressed, not just from the uncertainty of what was happening but also from being included with the Rebel team.

"You're where Ian wants you, Lydia. Trust me on this." Murphy smiled at her just as Nathaniel's fiancée, Elizabeth, a concert pianist, shifted the music closer to what Darcy and Doug had chosen.

Ian watched as Darcy paced in the small room at the church. Nerves, he thought.

"You're going to wear a hole in the floor, Darcy."

She smiled and kept walking.

"Doug's not running, but if you've talked to all the ladies and have refined how they did it, I can help you run. They'd never find you."

Darcy spun, mouth open, her long white lace-covered dress rustling softly. She went to speak, caught the spark of mischief in Ian's eyes, and shook her head.

"Not this time, Ian. Not this girl. My decision's made and he's waiting out there for me."

"You two make a great couple. Caleb said months ago you were a cute couple, or so I'm told."

She shook her head at him. "Thank you, Ian. You've helped to relieve the nerves. That was your intent all along."

Ian inclined his head, a smile in place. Darcy had asked him to walk her down the aisle and he had been honoured to do so. Her own family still shunned her, and she had been at a loss as to what to do, until she had looked up one day and saw Ian watching her.

A tap at the door, and Dave, one of the ushers, opened it. He nodded when he saw Darcy.

"You look beautiful, Darcy. Doug doesn't stand a chance."

She started laughing at him. "You two. I'll not make it down the aisle without laughing if you keep it up."

"They're ready for you, Darcy."

She tucked her hand into Ian's arm and moved forward, forward towards Doug, the man she loved more than anyone else. Doug turned, overcome by her beauty, then extended his hand to hers.

Ian slipped into the pew beside Lydia and reached for her hand, the slight roughness of his suit coat fabric rubbing her arm below her sleeve. Her nerves steadied at his touch and she relaxed, content to be by his side.

With Doug and Darcy on their way, the reception was winding down. Caleb stopped beside Abe, Hannah's hand in his. They spoke for a few minutes, before Caleb looked around.

"Where are Ian and Lydia?"

Abe nodded towards the window area. "They were there, but I think they've taken off. My guys are scattering for about a week or so before our next lot of trainees come in."

Caleb nodded. "Come see me on Monday, Abe, if you're around. Eddie and

Frankie have come up with some information I need to share with you."

Abe shot him a look, then nodded. "I will. Anything to be concerned about before then?"

Caleb shook his head. "They didn't seem to think so."

Abe turned to find Murphy standing behind him.

"Are you okay, Abe?" Murphy was picking up something from Abe, not quite sure what it was.

"I am, Murphy."

Murphy's head tilted and then he shook it. "No, you're not, Abe. What's up? And don't say it's to do with Ian and Lydia."

Abe shot Murphy a quick glance, then sighed. "No, it's not, Murphy. Days like this, they bring back a memory of what never happened for me." He clapped Murphy on the shoulder as he walked away.

Murphy stood and watched his friend, his heart breaking for him. Lord, he's hurting, and he's not sharing, so I have no idea how to help him. Touch him today, Lord.

Abe stood looking around his property later that day, then pulled out his wallet to remove a well-worn picture. I don't know where you are, Emma, but God knows. He has you in His hands. Lord, I just wish I knew what had really happened. It wasn't like Emma to do what she did. Movement beside him startled him. Rebecca stood there, eyes watching him, then glancing down at the photo.

"Oh, Abe!" Tears came to her eyes and she hugged her brother. "It still bothers you, doesn't it?"

"That it does, Rebel, that it does. I just wish I knew where she was, so I could talk to her."

Ian pulled his truck to a stop in front of the company hanger and turned to Lydia, watching her. She had changed from the soft yellow dress she had been wearing into jeans and a sweater.

Her eyes turned to him. "What are we doing here, Ian?"

Ian paused, suddenly unsure of himself. "This is our company hanger where we have our business jet. I also have my plane here."

"You have a plane, and you didn't tell me?"

"No, I guess it just never came up. I know I asked you to pack a bag for the week.

If you're willing, I would like to fly you to my parents. We can get away from all what's going on for a few days. I talked to your Dad. He says you haven't really taken any time off for months. You're not to report back for a week."

"A week? But what about you, Ian? Don't you work next week?"

Ian shook his head. "Not next week. Abe booked it off. So, will you join me?"

Lydia studied him, then turned to stare at the hanger. "I've never flown in a small plane before. I'm also not sure if I'm ready to meet your parents."

Ian laughed. "That's not a big deal. You're coming as my friend, and my friends have always been welcome."

Lydia turned to him, mouth open. Then she closed it as her eyes narrowed. "No, Ian, not just as your friend. How many times have you taken just one female home to meet your parents? We're working towards something between us. This is the next step, isn't it?"

Ian sighed. She had caught him out. "You're right. I should have talked to you, but I wanted to get you away from here for a few days." He turned his blue eyes to her. "So, will you? Mom and Dad won't bite."

She turned to stare out the truck window. This was something big that he was asking her to do. Was she ready for this step? She sighed and turned back to him. "All right, Ian. On to the next step. What do I do to help you get ready to fly?"

"Nothing but sit here and look pretty." He smiled at her look of outrage.

Chapter 22

66Mom! Dad! Are you around?" Ian opened the door for Lydia and ushered her in.

Ian's mother looked down the hall from the kitchen, wiping her hands on a towel, surprise on her face. Ian wasn't due to come home for a while.

"Ian! You're home! What are you doing here?" She approached to hug her son.

"Abe's given everyone the week off next week and I thought it would be nice to be at home."

"It's nice to have you here." She looked past him at Lydia. "And who do you have here?"

Ian reached a hand to draw Lydia forward. "Mom, this is Lydia Carmichael. I brought her home too as she hasn't had a holiday in months, her father tells me."

"You brought Lydia home, now did you? Welcome, Lydia." Ian's mother, Anna, reached out and hugged her, then with an arm around her shoulder, drew her towards the kitchen. "Your Dad's just gone to the store for me, Ian. He'll be back in no time." She seated Lydia at the round wooden table in the kitchen, then turned to put the kettle on. "You're just in time for tea, my lad."

"I was hoping we would be." Ian sat down beside Lydia and reached for her hand.

"Was today Doug's wedding?" Anna turned to study her son, finding him watching Lydia.

"It was, Mom. Everything went beautifully as you would say. Except Darcy refused to take me up on the offer to help her run away and hide."

"She did, did she? Well, I can't say as I blame her, Ian." A deep voice, similar in tone to Ian's, sounded from behind them. Ian was on his feet to greet his father.

"And who's your lovely young lady, Ian?"

Lydia turned as Ian's father approached her. "I'm Lydia Carmichael, Mr. Galbraith. I'm the one causing the problems."

"Causing problems? Not you, my dear. And it's Anna and Duncan, please."

Abe turned from looking out the front window of the police department building as he heard footsteps behind him. Caleb and Eddie walked towards him.

"Let's walk, Abe." Caleb nodded at the door. "We could all use some fresh air on this bright Monday morning."

As the three friends walked towards Mac's, Abe spoke. "You've found something?"

Eddie nodded. "We have, Abe. I had a team go out and search around the rocks once again behind your property. Murphy let them in. They've found some spots where a solitary camper was hiding from your view but where they could watch you. This has been in the last week to ten days, the team thinks."

Abe's steps slowed then stopped. "That close?" He stood for a moment, then walked forward. "Are they any closer to finding who it is?"

Caleb shook his head. "Not really. Whoever this person is, he is extremely careful. No garbage is left. Nothing other than some disturbed ground that isn't from an animal but a human."

"What about what's going on with Ian? Any closer to that?" Abe turned to stare at his uncle.

"Now that, we're making some progress on." Eddie waited until they were seated at a table in Mac's and their orders taken. "We've narrowed it down to three of the relatives Ian named. We're tracking them, but they have someone helping hide them. Word is out on the street we're looking for them and who they're after. We should hear something soon."

"I pray we hear something soon. The fellows are getting angry and I don't like them angry. This is the fourth one of them targeted."

Caleb nodded. "That it is. We'll have to see what we can do to keep the rest of you from being targeted, although you already are, Abe, and I wish I knew why."

"So do I, Caleb. I know I've made enemies over the years, all part and parcel of the job, but I can't pinpoint to one person."

The night before they were due to fly home, Ian stood with Lydia in the back yard of the home he grew up in. The air was scented with his mother's flowers and a slight breeze stirred the leaves. He reached to pull

Lydia into his arms. He watched the sunlight flickering across her face.

"Lydia, I was going to wait but I don't know if I can." He paused, searching for the words. "You are so beautiful. This last week has been wonderful, getting to know who you are. I have come to love you in a way I never thought I could love anyone."

She turned to search his face, waiting on what he would say. She wasn't sure if she was ready for it, though, it seemed too soon.

"Will you marry me, be mine for whatever time God grants us? Will you be the bride of my heart?"

She nodded. "God put us in circumstances where we had to get to know each other every quickly and on a level few people do. Yes, Ian, I will."

Ian drew her close to him and dropped his face to hers.

Duncan had been standing at the window and then turned to Anna. "You were right, Anna. They were ready."

Anna came towards Duncan and hugged him, as he dropped a kiss on her forehead. "They are just so right for each other. He steadies her, and she lightens him up." She turned and headed for the dining room. "This is certainly an occasion to bring out the good dishes, isn't it, Duncan?"

"That it is." Duncan paused, and then Anna heard him taking the stairs to the second floor. She smiled and nodded to herself as she knew what he had gone after.

Ian stood in the dining room a while later and looked around. "The good dishes, Mom? What's the occasion?"

Anna and Duncan shared a smile, then turned to the two standing together, Ian's arm tight around Lydia. "We were going to ask you that very question, Ian. Do you have something to tell us?" His mother's voice held a tremor and he wondered at that.

Ian glanced down at Lydia's face, then up at his parents. "I guess there is. I asked, and she said yes."

"And what was it you would have been asking, Ian?" Duncan's voice held a touch of amusement.

Ian shook his head at his father. "I asked her to be the bride of my heart, as you call Mom, and she has agreed."

Anna came to hug her son, then turned to Lydia. "Welcome to our family, Lydia. We have prayed all Ian's life just for you," she said as she hugged her.

Lydia's face showed her surprise and Duncan laughed as he too hugged her. "You see, Lydia, we prayed that God would bring just the right person for Ian at just the right time. You're it."

"You make it sound like we're playing tag or something, Dad." Ian's voice was amused as he claimed Lydia again.

"No games, Ian. None whatsoever." He stood and studied his son, grown tall and strong, and wondered where the years had gone. "Now, let an old man meddle for a minute. Have you decided on a ring or is that not on the radar yet?"

Ian and Lydia exchanged glances. "It's all so new, Dad, we haven't even talked about that." He looked up. "Why?"

Duncan pulled a small old-fashioned box from his shirt pocket. "Bear with me for a minute, you two. Lydia, you may not know that Ian is the only one of our four children who lived past early childhood. Our two girls and our other son lie buried in the church cemetery. Ian's grandmother was heartbroken, but Ian helped to fill the void they left, not that anyone could. Ian and his grandmother were great friends, part I think Ian because you're named for your grandfather. Just before Mom went home, she pulled her engagement ring from her finger and handed it to me, asking me to keep it safe for her wee Ian's bride." Tears in his eyes, he extended his hand with the box to Ian. "She would be delighted with your choice, Ian. Lydia reminds me of her."

Ian blinked to clear tears from his own eyes, thinking of his beloved grandmother, hearing once again the soft burr from the highlands in her voice, and knowing she would have loved his choice. He opened the box to find her yellow diamond ring. He turned to Lydia and started to speak.

Her fingers on his mouth, she nodded. "Ian, I would have no other ring. There's a history there that we need to remember, a love that we can share." She watched as Ian slipped the ring on her finger.

Later that night, she sought out Anna. "Anna, you and Duncan need to come to my home. I want you to meet Mom and Dad."

Anna turned from the counter where she had been working and searched Lydia's face. "We would be delighted to, Anna. And I do want you to do something for me."

"What's that?" Lydia was curious.

"Take me for a ride in that stock car of yours. I've always wanted to." The impish look on Anna's face sent Lydia into peals of laughter.

"That I can do, Anna. I'll even have my uncle Gregor and my brother Leigh get theirs out and we'll have our very own stock car race. Gregor owns part of the track, so that's not a problem whatsoever."

Anna reached to hug Lydia again. "I knew when I saw you that you would make life for us so much fun, and you will. Thank you, my dear."

Chapter 23

Murphy stuck his head into the office and eyed Abe as he sat at desk, deep in paperwork.

"Have you seen Ian?"

Murphy's question caught Abe off guard. "No, I haven't. Isn't he back yet? He said he'd be back by noon." Abe eyed the clock. It was now after 4 p.m.

"No. No one's seen him. I called the airport. He landed safely, put the plane in the hanger, and then he and Lydia left. That was before noon they said. I've checked with everyone I can think of."

Abe dropped his pen and stood. "I don't like the sound of this, Murphy. Ian would call if he had any problems. Has anyone received a call or text from him?"

Murphy shook his head. "No. Joseph and Matt are heading for the airport and then are going to try and trace where he went. I spoke with Lincoln. He hasn't heard from them either and neither has Gregor or Leigh. Leigh just got home late last night."

"Where's the rest of the team?" Abe walked out the door as he spoke.

"They're getting ready to head out to search. I'm with you."

Abe nodded, noting the men were pairing up as usual, but that Gideon had joined them. "Who's Gideon with?"

"Micah. He's driving the van as Micah works the computer."

"Good. We'll need him. Have you called Eddie or Frankie?"

"Luke made the call. To say they were unhappy was an understatement. They've gotten word that the three after Ian have picked up help somewhere along the line."

"That's not good. Let's go, Murphy. Where are we heading?"

"To Gregor's and then out from there."

Constant contact among the team members showed no sign of either Ian or Lydia. *Where are they, Lord,* Abe prayed. *Keep them safe, wherever they are. Lead us to them.*

Three days had passed and still no sign or word of the two. Eddie turned to study the white board in the conference. It held what little information that had been confirmed. They were growing desperate, he knew, needing information and not finding it. He turned as Frankie stopped beside him.

"What's the word on the street, Frankie?"

"Now that, Eddie, is strange. There's no word of where those two are. The word is that the three looking for Ian are still looking for him, but one source said they found him. I can't confirm that."

Eddie nodded. "I think that source is likely right. We should have found them by now. Both are too responsible not to have been in touch if they could have."

Frankie agreed. "I'll keep working the streets, Eddie. That's about all I can do. Our people here are digging deep. Tracker's hasn't come up with anything more for us either."

They both turned as Caleb spoke behind them. "We got this today in the mail. It's not the same as what we've had, and the lab doesn't think it's from the same people."

Eddie reached for the paper and read:

"We have your two friends. Expect a call from us at 7 p.m. Don't try to trace it or they're dead."

"No, I would say it's something taking advantage of rumours, and we get enough of those." Eddie stopped to think. "I just don't get it, Caleb. I just don't get why we can't find them or get any word on them."

"That's what has me worried, Eddie, that they're already dead and dumped somewhere and the people responsible have moved on." Caleb turned to walk away, a heaviness in his step they didn't see very often.

"That's what I'm afraid of, too." Frankie's voice was very quiet. He turned as an officer at the door called his name.

"Frankie, Abe's on line 1 for you."

"Thanks." He picked up the phone, expecting to hear the worst. "Abe, what do you have?"

"Matt just called. He's found Lydia and called in the paramedics. He didn't give a lot of details but asked that you meet him here." Abe's voice was tight with worry as he read off the address. "I'm headed that way now with Murphy. The other three teams are still searching."

Eddie's eyes watched Frankie's face as he was speaking. "Which one?"

"Matt found Lydia, and she's alive. Here's the address. It's way out in Taylor's Bush, isn't it? That's a strange place for her to be."

Eddie's hand stopped as he reached for the paper. "No, not really. Not if you wanted to hide someone. There are a lot of abandoned cabins out there. Who do we have we can get up in the air?"

"Sue's a pilot, but not for a chopper. Which would be better?"

"A chopper I think. I'll work on that, you head out."

Joseph stood near the entrance of the trail, waiting. He looked around, feeling the evil in the place. He shook his head. Lydia, dumped for dead once again. This time, too, they were in time, thanks to the hikers who had come this way and found her. He looked up as he heard the sirens and saw the flashing lights.

His heart sank as he saw who the paramedics were. The call had gone in for a paramedic, but they didn't realize that it would be Dave who responded.

Dave approached Joseph cautiously. "Joseph, you're here." He looked past him down the trail, heavy with brush and branches overhanging it.

"Dave. I was praying it wouldn't be you. We've found Lydia." He held out his hand to stop Dave. "She's alive. Matt's with her. He asked for a Stryker board and collar and a sheet."

Dave stared at him. "A sheet?"

Joseph nodded. "He wants to wrap her in a sheet for transport. That way, if there is any evidence on her clothes, we won't lose it."

Dave's face settled into new stern lines as it grew grim. "I didn't know there would be a problem."

"You hadn't heard that she and Ian have been missing?" When Dave shook his head, Joseph looked up to the sky. "They disappeared three days ago. They had flown back from Ian's home, and no one has seen or heard from them since."

"Take me to her." He reached for the kits he was handed. "Tom, we'll need the Stryker board, collar and a sheet."

Tom headed back for the items, not asking why. He had heard the conversation as he came up behind Dave. He nodded to Frankie as he walked towards Dave and Joseph.

"What do you have, Joseph?" Frankie's voice was grim.

"Not much evidence that we can see. We're going to wrap her in a sheet for transport and then you'll have that and her clothes. She's alive, but Matt doesn't know how bad she is."

"Any thoughts on what happened?" Frankie's questioned floated towards him as he led the way back to where Matt waited.

Joseph hesitated to speak, knowing Lydia's cousin and good friend was right behind him. "We think she either fell or was thrown from the back of a truck." He stopped and turned to face them. "Her hands were tied behind her, guys, so she had no way to protect herself when she went down. The heavy long grass helped to protect her when she fell."

Dave bit back words he really shouldn't say and then pushed by Joseph towards his cousin. Joseph looked after him and then back at Frankie.

"What else didn't you say, Joseph? What didn't you say that you should have to prepare Dave?"

Joseph shook his head. "She's pretty battered, Frankie, and Matt isn't convinced it's from her fall. He thinks the bruises are older than what they should be. It looks as if it might have been early this morning when she was dumped. One other thing. She still had a gag on her mouth."

Frankie stared at him, then down the trail. "Has Matt removed those?" he asked, afraid that Dave would find his cousin still bound.

"That's the first thing he did after he made sure she was still alive. He's set them aside in a safe place for you to have for evidence." Joseph turned to walk down the trail, Frankie on his heels. "Who does this, Frankie? Who treats a lady like that?" He paused, then continued. "One other thing. They must have gotten engaged. She's wearing a diamond ring."

Frankie shook his head. "That figures. All you guys do that, why would they be any different?" He turned at a noise behind him and saw the crime scene team coming along the path. "Anything else that struck you, Joseph?"

Joseph shook his head. "That's what we've found so far. Matt may have discovered more while I was waiting for you."

Matt looked up as he heard someone approaching, then rose to his feet, his eyes on Dave as Dave stopped feet from his cousin. Dave's face whitened, then hardened into grim lines.

"Talk to me, Matt. What do we have?" Eyes raised to Matt, he stared at him.

"So far, lots of bruising. I haven't moved her to her back yet, I was waiting for help. Just so you are aware, Dave, some of the bruising is older. I haven't touched her much other than to check for her vitals."

Dave nodded, then turned as he heard the rest approaching behind him. He nodded to the crime scene team, knowing they would need to do a preliminary check first before they could get to her. "Is it safe for them to go ahead, or do we need to transport first?"

Matt turned to watch the approaching figures. "If they're quick, we should be okay."

Frankie stood and watched as the team scoured the area for clues, then turned as Dave, Tom and Matt made ready to shift Lydia to the Stryker board. He shook his head, catching a glimpse of Joseph as he did so. He walked towards him.

"Talk to me, Joseph. You're deep in thought."

"It just strikes me odd that they would have them up here. Why? And where is God in all this? Things like this, they really try your faith."

"Eddie says there are a lot of abandoned cabins around here, but you're right, why here?" He turned as an officer approached. "You've gotten the statements from the hikers?"

"I have. They'll stop in on their way out to sign them. This kind of spoiled their day, so I'm heading back now to get them transcribed." Wilson, the officer, turned to watch the activity. "It baffles me, Frankie. This is a dead-end road. It only goes about another mile to mile and a half and then you're on foot."

Frankie turned to him. "You know this area that well?"

Wilson nodded. "We used to come up here camping and hiking when we were teens. The one cabin ahead would be my grandfather's, and it's not in that great a shape. I was up here about six months ago, and it was ready to collapse at that point."

"Here, draw me a map to where it is. When you get back to your cruiser, find

Eddie and Caleb and tell them what you've told me. We'll need to get a team together to go forward." As Wilson turned to leave, Frankie called after him. "When you're done, get back here. We can use you."

Chapter 24

Ian rolled awkwardly to his side from his stomach, head spinning as he did so. He had no idea what time it was or even what day. He knew it was daylight again, he could tell by the light hitting his eyelids. He cautiously cracked them open, and then closed them against the pain of the light. He slowly opened his eyes again, blinking to adjust his sight. He moved to sit upright and realized his arms were still bound behind him. They had finally removed his gag, but he still wouldn't tell them what they wanted.

Who are they anyway, Lord? And why me? Then, a thought hit him, and he searched the rundown cabin he was in. Lydia wasn't there. His eyes sliding shut, his heart raised in prayer that she was alive and safe, that she had managed to get away.

He slid towards a wall and using it as a brace, managed to get to his feet. Eyes searched for anything to cut his bonds, he stumbled around the cabin, kicking aside debris, finally finding a bottle he could drop and hopefully break. He dropped it and heard it smash. He dropped to his knees and then sat, feeling behind him for a shard of glass that would work.

It seemed hours later that he finally parted the last few strands of the rope, blood soaking his bonds. He could barely get his arms in front of him, reaching to rub his wrists, not caring at the hurt he felt. He sat for a minute to rest, then rose to his feet, searching the cabin and debris for any kind of weapon or food or water. Nothing! he thought. That figures. Now, if I only knew where I was I could get out of here. He stumbled as he crept towards the door hanging by one hinge and listened. He was alone.

Stepping out into the dimming light, his eyes probed the area, searching for his kidnappers, searching for any sign of Lydia. Nothing. He stumbled as he slowly moved forward, his head turning as he walked towards the sound of rushing water. That would help, he thought, if he could get some water. Lord, I need Your help right now. I have no idea where I am, but You do. Lead me home, please Lord, lead me home. Lead me back to Lydia.

Lincoln and Laurel stood uncertainly in the Emergency waiting room, the doctor heading their way. Leigh had dropped them at the door and gone to park their car. They didn't know this physician, but prayed he had good news for them.

"Mr. and Mrs. Carmichael, I'm Dr. Johns. Come, sit for a minute. I need to go over your daughter's injuries with you. Is her fiancé here?" His eyes searched their faces as they looked at each other in distress.

"I'm sorry, Dr. Johns. He's missing as well. The police tell us they think they were both kidnapped on Monday." Lincoln's voice broke as he spoke, and Leigh's hand came down on his father's shoulder.

The physician nodded. "All right, then. You'll be next of kin for now. She's in remarkable shape, actually. Bruising, some cracked ribs are the minor stuff. Her left shoulder took the brunt of the fall. We're waiting on imaging to be done, then we'll be sending her to the operating room for a look at it. The orthopedic surgeon doesn't think there's a lot of damage, but she does have a dislocated shoulder."

"One thing you need to be aware of, Doctor, is that Lydia doesn't handle any form of drug, painkiller or sedation well. Anything makes her sleep for days, even a small dose." Laurel's voice shook as she spoke.

"That's good to know. I'll make sure it gets passed on. Any other questions?" He searched their faces, then stood. "I'll come get you in a few minutes, and you can spend some time with her before we take her up to the OR."

Laurel and Lincoln sat back, stunned at what they had been told. Leigh looked up as Caleb approached and he went to meet him. A few minutes of quiet conversation and Caleb turned to leave, stopping as he saw the couple coming in the doors. Ian's parents, he thought, and went to meet them.

"Mr. and Mrs. Galbraith?" Caleb stopped in front of them.

"Yes, we are." Duncan's voice held a question.

"I'm Police Chief Caleb Logan, a friend of Ian's."

"Tell me, have you found him yet? We talked to Abe and he said Lydia was here."

Caleb shook his head. "No, but we have a good lead as to where he is, and teams are headed there now." He looked around. "Listen, Lydia's parents and brother are here. Come, I'll introduce you."

Anna shook her head. "No, Chief, we don't want to intrude."

"It's Caleb, and you won't be intruding." He stopped as he felt a hand on his shoulder. Lincoln stood beside him.

"I'm Lincoln Carmichael. You must be Ian's parents. Abe called to say you were on your way in. Come, join Laurel and I and Leigh." He led them over to where his family was sitting and waiting.

Caleb strode from the hospital, pulling his phone out as it rang. "What do we have?"

Eddie's voice was rushed. "Wilson just came in to finish the statements for those hikers and then he's heading back out. Frankie asked for teams to go up there and search. Sue's working on that right now."

"Wilson?"

"It's where his grandfather's cabin is. Frankie asked him to come back as he knows the area well. We don't have definite news that's where Ian is but we're working on that. Abe's pulling his men that way, too. Sue had the forestry chopper fly over but the pilot didn't see anything that raised an alert."

"Any more word on that letter we got?" Caleb checked his watch. They still had a few hours to go.

“Nothing. I think it’s a hoax to pull us off the hunt.”

“It could be, but we need to be prepared. Pull whoever you think is best on that and get them up to speed. I’m just leaving the hospital. Ian’s parents are here.”

“I heard from Abe they were on their way. How is Lydia?”

“Surprisingly well for what she’s been through. So far, Leigh says the worst injury she has is a dislocated shoulder.”

“Praise God for that.” Eddie’s voice faded for a minute, then came back stronger. “Wilson’s on his way back out. Where will you be?”

“At the office for now. I need to get together with our PR team and get some statements ready. Are you going to be there?”

Eddie paused, then spoke. “I can be, but I was thinking of heading over to the hospital.”

“Head there. They need someone with them and I want a police presence there. Take some officers with you. Call them in for overtime if we need to. We need a guard on Lydia’s room and also with their parents.”

Caleb pocketed his phone and looked around. He could feel the evil getting closer and he shuddered. Not knowing who was a problem. How could they deal with it when they didn't know who it was?

Abe stood watching as Frankie organized the search teams and then sent them out. He turned as he heard footsteps approaching from behind him. His team was here as was Gideon.

Frankie turned to speak to Abe just as gunfire rang out. They all ducked, then listened as chatter came across Frankie's radio.

"What's going on, Frankie?" Abe's voice sounded loud in the silence that now surrounded them. All the forest noise had gone quiet.

"One of the teams near the cabin just came under gunfire. They say we have a sniper." Frankie was talking as he moved towards the clearing ahead. "If we do, then we can't search until I get Doug and his team here with their sniper."

"Nathaniel's a sniper, Frankie, and our van with the gear is here."

Frankie stopped, then turned to search for Nathaniel. "That would work, except he's not an employee of the police department.

Yet." He beckoned Nathaniel forward even as he was asking their dispatch to put him through to Caleb on a separate frequency.

"Caleb, we have a situation. We've come under fire and we can't get our sniper here in a timely fashion, so we can search. Nathaniel's here." Frankie's eyes sought out Nathaniel's. "That's what my feelings are. Nathaniel, get over here and talk to Caleb. You'll have to share my mike."

Nathaniel listened intently as Caleb spoke rapidly, responding when he needed to. His team mates' eyes stayed on him, then flickered to one another, trying to determine what was up.

Nathaniel stepped back and turned. Frankie's hand on his arm came out to stop him as he went to move away. "It's just a temporary thing, Nathaniel, until we get this guy down. Then you can go back to being a civilian again. Get your stuff."

Nathaniel took off on a run as Abe turned to Frankie, eyes narrowing. "What did you just do, Frankie?"

"Caleb swore Nathaniel in on a temporary basis for the next twelve hours as an officer in our force. We need a sniper here and Doug's too far away to get here in time."

Abe nodded as he turned to see Nathaniel heading back their way. "All right, then let's get ourselves where we need to be."

"Be careful, guys. We have no idea where this person is. Night's closing in and I for one would like to see this wrapped up tonight. Nathaniel, you're set?"

Nathaniel nodded. "Do you have a spare radio, Frankie, or someone who can go with me to keep in contact with you?"

Frankie looked around at the officers standing, watching through the trees and brush towards the rundown cabin. "Wilson, get over here. You're with Nathaniel. He's one of Abe's men, but is on our force for a few hours. He's our sniper since we can't get Doug's or one of the others here in time."

Wilson shook Nathaniel's hand, and after a few minutes of quiet conversation, the two men moved off to the left. Nathaniel let Wilson lead, praying they could get there and disarm the sniper without killing him. He listened to the rustling on the forest ground, to the fluttering of the birds they disturbed. He shuddered for a moment, thinking of Ian being hurt and exposed to the elements. His eyes traced the sky. Bad weather was moving in.

Lord, we could really use some help right about now. I know You're here and in control, but please show us You. Nathaniel's words were unspoken, but he felt a peace flow through him as it did every time he prayed before he picked up his rifle. He had never ever had to use it. Would today be the first time he did, to protect a friend and fellow team member? Only God could answer that.

Lydia stirred, her eyelids flickering before staying open. She frowned, staring at the windows lining the wall beside her bed. Not again, she thought. Not in the hospital once again. She moved and whimpered with the pain from her shoulder. What did I do this time, Lord? What mess did I get myself into that landed me here?

She cautiously turned her head. Leigh was slouched in the chair beside her, her parents not in the room.

"Leigh." Her throat was dry, and she could barely articulate his name.

"Lydia. You're awake." Leigh was on his feet and bending over her bed. "Here, let me get you some ice chips. They don't want you drinking much yet."

"What happened?" She sought her brother's face, so much like their father's.

"You don't remember?" Leigh winced as she shook her head, then grimaced with pain.

"No. I don't. Where are Mom and Dad?"

"They went down to the cafeteria with Ian's parents to grab something to eat. You've been here for almost twelve hours."

"That long? I don't remember much about the last few days."

Leigh waited for her to ask about Ian, but she just laid there and stared across the room, expressions chasing across her face that he would like to know the meaning off. He wanted to be out there searching for the ones who did this, but he was needed here.

Her eyes finally settled back on his face. "He's dead, isn't he, Leigh? Ian's dead." Her voice held no expression.

"We don't know that, Lydia. Caleb and Abe are working on the premise that he's still alive. Are you telling me you saw him die?"

Lydia shook her head, blinking back the tears she refused to shed. "No, I didn't but I wasn't with him all the time." She sighed. "I guess now that I'm awake, they'll want my statement."

"They will. Eddie's here. He'll take it for you." Leigh pulled his chair closer to the bed and sat, hands grasping the bedside rail before he put his chin on his hands. "You know, you fought the nurses here."

"I what?" Lydia's voice cracked as she spoke. "Why?"

"They tried to take your ring off. You just curled your fingers tight and wouldn't relax them. Even unconscious you wouldn't let go of that connection to Ian." Leigh's eyes traced his sister's face.

She dropped her eyes to her hand and studied the ring. "It was his grandmother's, Leigh. His grandfather was an Ian too. She gave it to Ian's Dad for her "wee Ian's bride". I wish I could have met her."

"If she's like her son and grandson, she was a special lady." He turned at a sound came at the door. "Sounds like they're back. You can play possum if you like."

She smiled and shook her head at him and his reminder of what they used to do as children. "Not this time, Leigh. Go find Eddie for me. And by the way, Ian's mother wants to take part in a stock car race. She approached me on the sly that last night. I told her that between Gregor, you and me, we'd work that out for her."

Wilson halted just to the left of the cabin, eyes searching the dense brush on the other side. "Frankie, did anyone catch where the gunfire came from?"

"Negative, except from the other side of the creek. Do you see anything yet?"

"No. It's really grown thick in the last few years."

Nathaniel's eyes were roving the area, then dropped to the area along the creek. His heart stopped and then raced. He touched Wilson's shoulder and pointed.

"Frankie, we have a sighting on Ian. He's managed to get down by the creek, but with the sniper there, we can't get to him."

"Is he alive, can you tell?"

"Negative. We're too far away. We'll be off radio for a bit. I want to try and work our way closer to the other side." He stopped. "Hold everything, Frankie."

He silently pointed out an area to Nathaniel. Rifle raised, Nathaniel scoped out the area and then nodded. "There's our sniper, back far enough we can't get to him and right where he can take anyone out who tries to get down to Ian." Nathaniel's frustration was rising. "How do we draw him out?"

"Frankie, we spotted our guy. Almost directly across from the cabin, about 20 yards back into the bush. He's hidden well enough we can't get a shot at him."

Frankie turned to Abe. "They've found their sniper and they've found Ian."

"Is Ian alive?" Abe could hear the men behind them holding their breath. They had been hurt, beaten up on and by missions, but never once had they ever lost anyone, team mate or those they were protecting.

"They can't get close enough to tell. Matt, Dave's back by the vehicles. Head back there and grab what you need and bring Dave and Tom back up here. That way you'll be close when we need you." Frankie's eyes assessed each one, seeing the determination to bring Ian out alive in each of them.

Frankie's remaining officers spread out around the clearing area, some managing to make their way close to the creek.

"What are you seeing? Anyone?" Frankie waited for a response.

"I've got him in my sights, Frankie, but he's just a little too far for me to take out, and I'm not sure I can get any closer." Nathaniel's voice came back over the radio. "Ian's moving, guys. He's alive. If he only stays down."

Abe and the rest of his team breathed easier. Now they just had to get to him.

"How do we get to him, Frankie?" Abe's mind was racing. How did they do it? The team had faced something like this in the past and managed to get their client out alive, but this was different. Here they had other men to consider, who didn't know how they worked. He turned as Matt came back up behind him. "He's alive, Matt. We just have to figure out how to get to him."

Matt nodded, his mind whirling with thoughts and plans. Like Abe, he knew if it was just his team mates they would be in and out, but with the unknown around them, they just couldn't take a chance.

Lydia turned to watch her mother, sitting next to her, her head down as she read. Lydia's mind was clearer, the pain from her shoulder less. Her eyes dropped to her left hand and the ring Ian had placed there. Lord, please bring him back safely and alive. If not, then give me the peace and grace I'll need. She felt a presence beside her and looked up to see Anna standing there.

"Do you need anything, Lydia?" Anna's voice held a stronger burr of the highlands that night, evidence of the stress she was under.

"No, Anna, I'm fine. Just praying."

Anna's hand came out to lay gently on Lydia's head. "We all are praying the same way, Lydia, but I think you've reached a new level that we haven't gotten to yet."

Lydia nodded, tears sparkling in her eyes. "I have, Anna, but I know God will avenge no matter what happens."

Anna's eyes sought those of Laurel and saw the dawning comprehension in Laurel's eyes. They both knew what they wanted, but they had to be ready to let Ian go and let God fulfill whatever plan He had in place.

"Can you help me sit up more, please Mom?"

"They don't want you to yet, Lydia."

"I don't care. I want to sit up and if you don't help me, then I'll do it myself."

A hand on her good shoulder stopped her. "Lydia, please, you need to do exactly what you're asked. They warned us that if you try moving around too much over the next few hours, you might undo the repair. And that means taking you back to the operating room. That you won't like. You know you can't take the medications they need to give you." Laurel's voice was pleading with her daughter.

Lydia sighed. "You're right, Mom. I need to be patient, and it's too hard."

Chapter 26

Nathaniel could hear vague chatter coming over Wilson's radio as he searched for a better spot to take aim from. He had never ever had to use his sniper skills in all the years he had been on Abe's team. Then he saw what he wanted. A more sheltered area for them, where they could cover the men as they went in to get Ian.

"Wilson, down there. By those rocks. If we can get down there, between us and your other officers, we might be able to get in enough gunfire that we can cover Matt and Dave getting in and getting out."

"Are you crazy?" Wilson couldn't believe what he was hearing.

"No. I'm serious. Matt's been under fire in almost similar situations before. Dave's served a tour overseas as a medic. You can bet he's been under fire many times. Talk to Frankie or let me."

Wilson's disbelieving eyes stared at Nathaniel. Then he relayed what Nathaniel had said.

"Frankie, it will work. My team goes in for cover too, down with Matt and Dave. They snatch Ian and we draw back."

Like Wilson, Frankie was not sure of what he was hearing. "Abe. It won't work."

"Trust me, Frankie. We've done this before, almost an identical call to this. We can do it."

Frankie drew a deep breath and thought. They didn't have many options and night was closing in. Who knew how long Ian would last, out in the elements overnight?

"If anything happens to you, I'm not responsible."

"Give us ten minutes to get back with our gear. Scrape that," Abe commented as he turned and was handed his gear. "My guys were prepared. Ask them where's the best way for us to get down there."

Wilson appeared at that moment. "Follow me, I'll get you down there. And for the record, I don't like this. You're putting everyone at risk."

Abe shook his head. "So, leave then. We've done this so many times, we could do this in our sleep. It's what we do, Wilson. It's who we are."

Abe followed Wilson back to where Nathaniel had tucked himself in by the rocks, the rest of the team behind him. A few quiet words among themselves, then the team spread out, Matt and Dave getting as close as they could to Ian, twenty feet separating them from him.

"It's getting dark, Abe. We'll have a better shot at getting him out when it's dark. Chances are he doesn't have night vision gear."

"I pray you're right, Nathaniel. Matt's ready to go in when I give the word." Abe's eyes searched for each of his men, knowing they would be in place and ready to act. "I pray we don't have to kill anyone, Nathaniel. We've never had to yet."

Nathaniel shook his head. "It's been close a few times, but I don't know if we've ever been under the kind of pressure we are today."

Abe shook his head. "We haven't. It's never been one of us we're trying to rescue. Ian's usually the one leading in this and now we're having to work without him."

Night crept in closer and then it was dark. Nathaniel adjusted his night vision goggles and studied the area they had tracked the man to.

"He's still there, but he's not able to see. He doesn't have the goggles." Nathaniel's eyes swept the area. "Get Matt ready to go. Any time now."

Abe gave a quiet command to Matt, and then watched as Matt and Dave crawled towards Ian, stopping every few feet to watch and listen. Finally, a breath of relief as they reached him.

"This is where it gets tricky, Abe. Once they start to move backwards, he may see them, and we'll be into a shooting match."

Nathaniel's eyes strayed back to where the man's form was. Then his eyes stopped.

"Abe, something's off. Get Matt and Dave out with Ian now. I'm not sure what's going on over there, but something has changed."

Abe barked an order to Matt and together he and Dave scooped Ian up and made a run for shelter, expecting any moment to feel bullets hitting them.

Abe stared at them, then across the creek, then back at Nathaniel. "What just happened?"

"I'm not sure. Abe, but we need to move in on him. I think someone took him out. His position has changed, and his rifle is pointing down. He doesn't seem to be moving at all."

Wilson was communicating with Frankie. "Frankie wants to know what you see."

"Tell him to hold on. We're moving in and if he has a problem with that, he can take it up with me afterwards. This is what our training is all about. We've been in this kind of situation more than any of your officers."

Wilson could hear Frankie in the background as he listened to Abe. "Frankie, Abe's moving in. He said for us to hold tight."

"I don't like it, Abe, but go ahead."

Abe and his men crept closer, moving silently, Nathaniel standing guard with his sniper rifle up and ready. He lowered it when he saw Abe stand back up from the man and then turn and walk away.

"Abe, what's up?" Nathaniel asked as he walked towards him.

"He's dead, Nathaniel, and just in the last hour we think. Someone got to him."

"Who?" Nathaniel's eyes probed the area. "I didn't see anyone." He turned as Frankie approached. "We didn't shoot him, Frankie."

"I know you didn't, Nathaniel. Did you guys see anything at all?"

Both shook their heads. "None of us did. Whoever it was has to have come up behind him."

"Wilson, what's the terrain like over there?"

"About the same as here. Lots of game trails one can follow. You won't be able to do much before morning."

Frankie nodded. "We'll have to leave it until then. Wilson, you're one who'll be staying here to guard. Pick three you want with you." He watched as Wilson moved away. "Now isn't this a fine kettle of fish, as my granddad would say."

Abe nodded, then spoke. "If you don't need us right now, we're off with Ian to the hospital."

Frankie looked around. "How is he, have you heard?"

"Not yet. Matt hasn't said anything."

"Go then. Caleb said Eddie was at the hospital earlier. He has guards on Lydia and her folks. Ian's folks are there as well."

Abe caught up with Matt and Dave as they worked on Ian in the ambulance. He watched with steady eyes but quaking heart.

How is he, Lord? How many more of my guys are going to be hurt like this?

"Talk to me, Matt. How is he?"

"He's in rough shape, Abe. We're almost ready to transport." Matt looked up, a heaviness in his face. "Pray he makes it, Abe. He's been beaten pretty bad, and then been out in the elements for who knows how long."

Abe turned to his men. "I'm riding shotgun. Meet us there." Abe moved to close the doors of the ambulance, then around to climb in beside Tom. Tom shot him a quick glance, then with siren blaring and lights flashing, he took off for the hospital, full police escort in place. Abe stared out the side window, his thoughts tracing the years he had known Ian. Lord, I don't want to lose such a good friend. Work a miracle please.

Abe's men milled around the Emergency Room waiting area and back and forth from the outdoors. Their faces were grim and their stance stern. Eddie walked towards Abe, who looked up as he approached.

"Walk with me, Abe." Eddie turned without waiting for his nephew to answer. "Talk to me. Tell me what happened."

Abe talked it through with Eddie. "I don't know what we could have done different, Eddie. It's so bizarre."

Eddie looked behind him as he heard footsteps approaching. "I don't think you could have done anything different. Here's Caleb. Tell him exactly what you told me."

Abe turned as his friend approached and Eddie walked away. Caleb assessed him in the bright lights of the parking lot.

He's taken a real beating tonight, Lord, and he needs Your comfort. All his guys do. Guide the medical staff as they treat Ian.

"What happened, Abe? Frankie gave me what he had."

Abe shrugged. "I've given a statement to Eddie. But I really don't know what happened. Nathaniel had him in sight the whole time and saw nothing happen to him. Who got him?"

"We'll go in once daylight comes and see what we can find. Frankie didn't have much more information than you did." Caleb stopped speaking for a moment, staring across the parking lot. "You really threw Frankie tonight, you know. He's never seen your team in action."

"I know he hasn't. It's about time he did. You have, so you know what we did."

Caleb nodded. "I know, and I know it's the only way you could have gotten to Ian so quickly. Talk will come up, it always does. I'll get our PR people to put out a statement. That'll take care of that." He hesitated, then spoke again, "Now, about Ian. Have you heard anything?"

Abe's steps turned back to the hospital. "No, I haven't yet. His parents are here, Eddie says."

"They are. They've been with Lydia's folks all day. I've had a guard posted with them and with Lydia."

Chapter 27

Abe watched as the Emergency Room physician spoke with Ian's parents. He would talk to them later, but for now, he sat by himself and watched. Rebecca sat down beside him, her hand reaching for his.

"Have you heard anything yet, Abe?"

"Not yet. I'll go talk to his dad in a bit. Right now, they need to digest what they're being told."

"What did Matt say?"

Abe tilted his head to study his sister. "Not a lot, Rebel. Not a lot. He was too anxious to get him here. He and Dave were working on him when we rolled out." His eyes strayed to where Gideon was standing with Micah. "Your guy was a lot of help and support today, Rebel."

"I know. I worried so much about all of you." She sat back, eyes roaming the room. "Caleb's got a lot of officers here, doesn't he?"

"He will have until he can find out who did it and why." Abe reached for his sister's hand. "Why don't you and Gideon head out?"

She shook her head. "Not until we have word, Abe. Ian's family."

Abe nodded, then rose as Duncan walked towards him.

"Duncan, how is he?"

Duncan looked around, then pointed towards the cafeteria. "I'm told, late as it is, we can still get a coffee and something to eat. I need to do something to keep busy, and that will help. Come with me."

Abe watched as Duncan rolled the heavy china cup between his hands, not saying anything, just waiting for Duncan to speak.

"Thanks for getting in and getting him out, Abe." Duncan finally looked at Abe, a combination of worry and gratitude on his face.

Abe shrugged off the thanks. "He's one of us, Duncan, not just a team member but a good friend to us all."

Duncan nodded. "I know that, Abe, but for you to have risked your lives to get him and bring him back to us, that's something we'll never forget."

Abe looked down for a minute, embarrassed at the thanks. "What have the doctors said about his condition?"

"Not a lot yet. They're assessing him, were waiting for blood work and imaging results. They did say he wouldn't have lasted through the night, not out in the elements." He gave a half smile. "Lincoln told Lydia that Ian was safe and downstairs in Emergency. They almost had to tie her down to keep her in her bed."

"They're quite a pair, those two. They bring out the best in each other."

"They do. We were blessed to have both of them with us last week." Duncan studied the younger man in front of him. "Don't blame yourself, Abe. There's nothing you could have done to prevent this."

Abe shrugged. "May be not, but there is someone there that has targeted me and is trying to get to me through my men. I take responsibility for that."

"We know you do, Abe. That's what make you the leader you are." Duncan looked away, then looked back. "We have been praying for you for years, Abe. I know there's something else going on with you.

The Lord has told me that much. I don't know what it is, but you are prayed for."

Abe looked up, ready to thank him and saw Matt headed his way. "Duncan, here comes Matt. You haven't talked to him yet tonight, have you?"

"No, and I would like to."

Matt seated himself beside Abe and said something quietly to him. Abe nodded and then stood to walk away. He stared down at Duncan, then his eyes flicked up. "Duncan, stay with Matt while you're here. We've gotten word that the men who took Ian are somewhere near here. There are men with Anna and also Lydia's folks."

Abe strode away, grimness in his bearing. This is not what they needed, to have an armed standoff or shootout on hospital grounds. He went looking for Eddie.

"Eddie, what do we have that we can help you with?"

Eddie turned. "Matt found you. What we need is for your guys to provide security for Ian's people, Lydia and her people. We have an officer with Ian right now and one outside his door, although Murphy refuses to leave his side."

Abe smiled. "Murphy and Ian are good friends. That doesn't surprise me. Let him stay. An extra body may be what we need there. Have you gotten any word on how he is? Duncan didn't say much."

Eddie nodded, pausing to sort through all that was running through his mind. "He's in rough shape, Abe. They have said he wouldn't have lived until morning. Dehydration. Exposure. He's was beaten pretty bad and that blunt force trauma has led to some internal injuries. Fractured ribs and one pierced his lung." Eddie caught the look on Abe's face. "No, it didn't happen when Matt and Dave moved him. It happened a day or so before that. They're amazed he survived."

"God again, Eddie. I pray His justice is served and He avenges how our people were treated." He turned to study the waiting room once again. "Matt said you had word that these guys were near here."

"That's what we've been told. Wilson is anxious for morning to come so he can search the area."

"I can tell you what he'll find. Nothing. Absolutely nothing. The gun used would have had a silencer on it. Nathaniel was watching the whole time and saw nothing out of the ordinary."

"You know, that's what bothers me. You had the guy under surveillance and he still got killed. Who snuck up on him, right under your noses?" Eddie went silent, pondering on what had happened. "Was it one of the ones after Ian or the one after you? The only ones after Lydia are those after Ian."

Abe nodded. "That's the problem I see. Which one?" He turned to face Eddie, a question on his face. "I have still to figure out who's after me and why they're going after my team."

"They're going after your team as a warning and also as a way to get to you. You show how you feel about your men in the way you interact with them and treat them. Anyone who is around you much notices that."

"So, are you saying it's someone I know, who gets close to me?"

Eddie shrugged. "We don't know. We're still working on that on the side. But right now, let's head back in and see what the status is on Ian."

Rebecca was headed towards him as they walked back inside. She reached to hug her brother as his eyes searched the room, noting the grim look on his team's faces. Then his eyes sought Duncan and Anna, who sat in what he thought was shock.

"Rebecca, talk to me. What's going on?" Abe hugged his sister, his voice low and gentle.

"They're taking Ian to surgery. They've found some bleeding, I think they said the spleen or kidney or something. I can't remember. He's critical, Abe. They told his parents he might not come through, given the shape he's in right now."

Abe hugged his sister even harder as tears clouded his eyes. Rebecca was taking it hard. She treated each one of the men like a brother, but Ian was special to all them in a way they couldn't define.

"Come, let's find Gideon and then the chapel. We'll spend the time in prayer." Abe led his sister away as Eddie turned back to leave the room again, phone out to call Caleb. It just might be a murder investigation after all.

Chapter 28

Looking around at the men and women gathered in the surgical waiting room, the surgeon sought for Ian's parents. He crossed quietly to stand before them. Then he crouched down in front of them, his hand reaching out to touch Anna's hand. She started and looked at him in apprehension, Duncan's arm tightening around her.

"Mr. and Mrs. Galbraith, Ian's in recovery right now. It took a while, but we were able to stop the bleeding. I wouldn't go into the details, but he wouldn't have lasted much longer out there. His friends got him here in time. He should recover without any problem." He watched with compassion as Anna's eyes shut and tears slid down her face. He looked up at Duncan with a question on his face.

"It's like this, doctor. We lost three children before they were three, two girls and a boy. Ian's our survivor. God's not done with him yet, by the looks of it."

The surgeon nodded. "I can see that. We felt your prayers over the hours we were in surgery. It was one of his team mates that challenged a friend of mine to find God not long ago, so I know what you've been doing while we're been working." He stood, then held out his hand to shake Duncan's. "Give us a couple of hours and we'll have Ian to an ICU room, and a nurse will come find you. You can see him then. I understand his fiancée is anxious to see him as well. We'll see what we can arrange for that." He turned and walked away, humbled by the feeling that it hadn't been him operating but God.

Abe watched, then rose and walked over to Duncan, sitting quietly beside him, waiting for him to speak. His heart opened up to God, asking for healing, for peace, for justice.

Duncan finally turned to Abe. "It's good news, Abe. He's in recovery now. The doctor said they could find the bleeding and stop it." Duncan had to stop, overcome with emotion. "Once again, thank you for bringing our son back to us."

Abe nodded, unable to speak. He laid his hand on Duncan's shoulder, then stood walking to where the team had gathered, apprehension in their bearing.

"He's in recovery, guys. He's going to make it." He could see the relief flowing through each one. "I'm staying for a while. If any of you want to head out, go ahead. Matt, Nathaniel, thank you for what you did tonight. Ian wouldn't be here if it wasn't for you. Joseph, Luke, Murphy, Micah, you guys. I don't know what to say. You were willing to go under fire to get him. That's what makes us a team. Go on. Go get some rest." Abe turned and walked away, once more heading for the chapel.

Lydia roused as she felt a hand on hers. Her father stood beside her bed. She could see tears in his eyes and started to shake her head.

"No, Dad. Don't tell me." Her voice shook with emotion.

"No, it's not what you think, honey. Ian's alive and is now in an ICU room. If you're up to it, I have a wheel chair here. The surgeon's said for you to come spend some time with your beau. It can't be a long time, but he's okayed it. His parents have been in with him and have said you need to come." He held his daughter as she sobbed, then helped her into a robe, tucking a blanket around her once she was in a wheelchair. He nodded to the officer standing outside her door as he headed for the elevator.

Lydia watched Ian's face as she sat beside him, her hand on his. Thank you, Lord, you've brought him back. Heal him. Let the culprits be found and punished.

She turned her head slightly as steps came up beside her and then Duncan's hand was laid on her shoulders.

"He's back, Lydia. He's come back to you." Duncan's voice was thick with emotion.

"God brought him back to all of us, Duncan. He wasn't ready for him to come home yet. He's still needed here on earth."

"He's found a very wise young lady in you, Lydia."

"He's helped me to grow in many ways, Duncan. Last week, it was wonderful just to spend time getting to know one another. Having you and Anna as part of it was wonderful as well, getting to know the parents who raised the man I love."

Duncan swallowed back his emotions. "When you're ready, Lydia, call us Mom and Dad, or whatever variation of that you'd like. You're family. Anna is delighted to finally have a grown-up daughter, even if she has to share her, and I am too." He dropped a kiss on her cheek and then turned to walk away.

Lydia's voice came to him quietly. "Thank you, Dad. I would be honoured to call you Mom and Dad."

Duncan swallowed back the tears and nodded as he walked away. Thank you, Lord, for these two.

A week later, the head of his bed raised, Ian watched Lydia as she wandered his hospital room, checking for dead flowers in the bouquets, straightening the cards, generally putting in time. He was to be discharged on the following day, and he knew Lydia was unsure of what lay ahead of them. He finally held out his hand.

"Lydia, come here." She stopped, not looking at him. "Lydia, sweetheart, come here. Talk to me."

She turned, and he sighed. "Come here. Tell me why the tears."

She sat beside him on the bed. Not satisfied, Ian reached and drew her up beside him, cuddling her close in his arms, mindful of the sling on her arm. "Talk to me. Please. Don't shut me out."

"I just question why. I know I shouldn't, but I do."

"Where does it say we can't ask why? Can you quote me chapter and verse?" She shook her heard. "I'm sure even David questioned God. Read through some of his Psalms. You get that impression that he questioned, even as he acknowledged the sovereignty of God. We wouldn't be human if we didn't ask that. We just have to not dwell on it and stay there, but reach out for God's hand that's outstretched for us."

"I know that, Ian. I just find it hard to accept at times. I see it when we go work disasters. I hear that question asked, the why me's, the why not me's." She laid her head on his shoulder. "I guess I'm just trying to make sense of this whole mess, not knowing who it was." She tilted her head to look up at him. "Has Frankie said anything about who?"

Ian shook his head. "They're still working it through." He stopped, his eyes on her. "Listen. They're letting me out tomorrow."

"I know. Your mom's anxious to get you home."

Ian smiled. "Well you see, that's the problem. They don't have a home to go home to right now."

"What do you mean?" She stared at him, startled. "What happened to their home?"

"Mom said they decided that as this was home for you and me, they just had to move here too."

"Oh Ian. They did?"

"They're going to be house hunting here." He watched as she thought it through.

"They can come stay at my house. You should too, until you're ready to move back to your place. I'll move back in with Mom and Dad while you're there."

He dropped a kiss on her head. "Thank you, sweetheart. Not many would do that."

He looked up as the door opened and a stranger entered.

"Can we help you?" Ian tensed, something warning him about the stranger.

The stranger watched the two of them before he approached the bed. His hand came out and a weapon was pointed at them. "Tell your woman to get out of here, Galbraith. This is between you and me."

"No. I'm not leaving, Ian. He won't let me now that I've seen him. He has to get rid of me too, if that's what he's planning on doing with you."

The stranger laughed, a hard, harsh laugh. "Don't say I didn't give a chance,

Galbraith." He pointed the weapon at Ian's head. "It's time to settle a score."

"Do I know you?" Ian was puzzled. As far as he knew, he had never seen this man before.

"Oh yeah, you do. Back when we were teenagers, you walked away from my brother. He ended up in prison because of you."

"Your brother? Who's that?" Then comprehension dawned on Ian. "Your brother, Wayne. He deserved what he got. I had nothing to do with that."

"Oh yeah you did. If you had still be with them, they wouldn't have gotten caught."

Ian shook his head. "Sorry, buddy, that's not how it works. They made their choices and it was to stay on the wrong side of the law. I'm not responsible for that."

Lydia watched as the man's visage changed and became haunted and hate filled. Oh, Ian, she prayed, please don't aggravate him more than he is She watched as the door opened in a quiet manner. Frankie slipped in.

Ian's eyes never wavered from the man in front of him. "So, it's been you all along has it?"

"Sure, it has been. Me and my sister and her husband. We wanted you to pay. He died a year ago during a riot in the prison he was sent back to. So, you see, you're responsible."

"And you're the ones who kidnapped this woman earlier and dumped her?"

"We sure are. We're going to make sure you both pay."

"And those devices and tracker on my vehicle? That was you?"

The man nodded. "Yeah, it was. Except it didn't work out the way it was supposed to."

"What about the car that trailed us that day? Was that you?"

The man shook his head. "Nope, not us. We wouldn't have just trailed you. We'd have run you off the road. Now you pay, you and your woman."

Frankie's weapon touched the man's ear. "I think not. Now lower your weapon. You're not going to make anyone pay. Your sister's husband is dead, she's in custody. She told me where to find you today."

An officer moved up beside the man and disarmed him, then handcuffing him, led him from the room.

"Haven't you two had enough excitement to last you for a while?" Frankie's tone had changed to an amused one.

"I have. I don't know about Lydia, though." Ian's tone was teasing as he hugged Lydia closer to him. Then turning serious, he asked, "Is that all of them now?"

Frankie nodded. "All the ones after you. We still haven't figured out who killed the sniper waiting for us. I don't know that we will. But these three were responsible for what you two went through. When they stopped you on the road that day, Ian, they had hired a couple of men to help. Those two men disappeared very quickly afterwards. We can't track them down anywhere."

"So, we don't get all the justice some people think we deserve."

"Not really. But I can tell you what happened after you were kidnapped. They held you in a house in town for about two days, then headed out to the cabin. They were planning on leaving both of you there, but the one that left, he had the idea that if he threatened Lydia again, you'd cave and agree that you were at fault for his brother's death. It seems that as he was holding her up, the driver hit a rock or bump in the road and

Lydia fell out. They figured she was dead or would die and didn't bother to even check on her. The sister's husband was holding you down in the truck bed, Ian, so you couldn't get up to help Lydia.

"The sister has also admitted to kidnapping Lydia previously and drugging her, not realizing the effects the drugs would have on her. They really thought she was dying and came up with the plan to frame you for her death by having you at the marina about the time she was dumped." Frankie shook his head. "They certainly didn't plan well."

"I'm just glad it's all over with, Frankie." Lydia finally spoke. "Now that they're in custody, we don't need a bodyguard anymore? We can go home?"

"You can." Frankie turned to walk out the door. "I have some people waiting out here. I'll stall them for a minute or two, but I can't stall them for long." His laughter trailed behind him as Ian's head bent over Lydia's.

Epilogue

Ian went looking for Lydia in the house his parents had bought from her. She wasn't to be found. This was not how he had planned to spend the day, searching for his fiancée.

Then he stopped. She was in the back yard, bent to smell the roses his mother had planted when Lydia let them have the house during his recovery. She had known then that she would let them have the house.

He opened the storm door and walked slowly towards her. They had been through a lot, these two, but it had brought a stronger bond between them. But Ian knew without a shadow of a doubt life would be boring and less than what it could be without God's chosen mate for him in it.

Lydia turned as she heard the soft footsteps behind her and smiled. Ian was the man God had chosen for her, the image of who she had dreamed about and prayed for. She reached for his hand.

"Ian. You're back. It didn't take your team long."

"No, it was a quick in and out recovery for us. No danger at all this time."

"I'm so glad." She looked up at him from the circle of his arms. "Our plans are coming together, dearest."

"What plans would they be?" Ian kept the smile off his face, but the twinkle in his eye gave him away.

"You know quite well what plans. Abe's been good about the cabin. Joshua and Leith have worked their magic once again." She laid her head on him. "I'm so glad you survived our adventure, dearest."

"That was quite the adventure we had. Let's never do that again, okay?" He leaned back a bit, so he could look down into her face. "Now, how be we go out for a nice romantic dinner, just us two, and you can tell me about the plans you have that are coming together?"

"I would like that. Ian, do you think God avenged Himself with those men and that woman?"

Ian shrugged. "I don't know, Lydia, but He does. We just need to keep our eyes on Him. He looks after the details for us."

"I like that thought, Ian, that we don't have to worry over the details, that we don't have to worry about revenge, that God is so big yet so small, and that He is involved in each detail of our lives."

Ian traced her face with his finger. "I have a preacher for a girlfriend. Who would have thought? But I agree totally with you." His head bent over hers as he claimed her mouth. Raising back a bit, he said, "Don't ever change."

Dear Readers

Thank you for choosing to read the story of Ian and Lydia. Ian, the quiet one of the team, who everyone wants as a brother, met his match in the spitfire and fun-loving personality of Lydia.

How God protected them and led them down the road from wanting revenge to letting Him avenge is the premise of the story. How many times have we wanted to avenge ourselves or someone we love, have wanted revenge? We need to let God have that. His plans include that.

Where are you in your walk with God? It is a daily struggle to keep ourselves where we need to be. My prayer for each reader is that you will let yourself be open to God, open to His leading, open to the plans He has for you. He wants good for you, not evil.

God bless each one of you.

Ronna

www.ingramcontent.com/pod-product-compliance
Lightning Source LLC
Chambersburg PA
CBHW070451200726
48293CB00007B/2164